People are Strange

PERIPETEIA   PRESS

Published by Peripeteia Press Ltd.

First published: September 2021 ISBN: 978-1-913577-07-0

For Fergus, Corrinne and Naomi, with love. And to my mother, with thanks.

Contents

All these things entered you
As if they were both the door and what came through it.

Seamus Heaney, *Markings*

Match of the Day

1

The sound of a TV news report is playing quietly in the background. He cannot hear exactly what is being said and he's not really listening because he might not understand it anyway. He's excited though because he's allowed to stay up late, the football will be on soon and he's hoping United will be the featured match.

When he next looks at the screen, there's a large, brown-grey mansion, surrounded by trees, pine trees maybe, in the foreground and a snow-capped, misty mountain looming up behind. Lots of cars are parked outside, so, he thinks, the building might be a hotel. A montage of short, quick scenes follows, each fading to black: a large living room with roaring fire; a long corridor with brightly coloured party balloons outside the doors. Something about it all, its strangeness, arrests his attention. The camera slowly zooms and sweeps across mysteriously empty interior spaces.

It's Saturday night, the one night when he's allowed to stay up much later than normal, past ten o'clock. As long as he's ready for bed straight afterwards and no complaining, mind, or wheedling to stay up any later. He's already in his pyjamas to facilitate the swift transition required from lounge to bed. Mum's in the kitchen somewhere, making a cup of tea. As usual, dad's in his favourite chair, reading the weekend paper, totally absorbed.

What is that? It's almost a white-out. Snow. He can make out a lamp post and maybe some kind of snow vehicle behind. Everything's so bluey grey, it's really hard to see what's really going on.

Dad and him make sure they never find out the scores, in the football; it's a solemn pact between them. Makes it more exciting, the not knowing.

Especially, for him, if United are playing, though dad supports City. He really hopes United will be the main match. He's been keeping his fingers crossed they've won.

There's no music. Normally there's music with this sort of thing. Almost silence. He doesn't really know what sort of thing this is. It might be a trailer for a film.

Starksy and Hutch, with Huggy Bear and that great red car with the bold white tick down the side has just finished and whatever this is is about some other programme coming on later when he'll be tucked up safely in bed. Something inexplicable that adults watch. One day he'd like to be like Hutch. Blond and handsome, Hutch even looks a little bit like dad, which means he will also look a bit like him too when he grows up. Hutch always wears a cool, tan brown leather coat, an open shirt, faded jeans, pumps. He's a tough good guy and he cracks jokes. His older cousin also has a bit of the Hutch about him and drives a Capri whose lozenge shape reminds him of Hutch's car.

Now there is a car, travelling up a windy mountain road. Maybe going to the hotel. Off on holiday, maybe. Dad's paper is so big he can't see any of him, apart from the legs below and the furry brown slippers that always make him think of bears.

A thick-set figure is framed in silhouette. He thinks it's a man, but it's hard to tell. Hunched over and he's coming out of somewhere in the

—

gloom. From a garage is it? In front are streetlamps and a building obscured by mist, like in a ghost story. The figure is carrying something in his two hands. It is a large axe. Suddenly he hobbles forward into a dip in the snow and then moves quickly, lumbering unevenly towards the building.

He takes a tentative bite of one of his digestive biscuits. He has three in his favourite small silver bowl. Because it's Saturday night, he's also allowed a fizzy drink too. But not coke, because that might keep him awake, apparently. He only nibbles a tiny bit of digestive and only takes a sip of the lemonade because he's not supposed to drink it too quickly - it gives him hiccups if he drinks too quickly - plus he's trying to save these treats from when the football starts.

A flash of white. Weird, eerie music starts up. Suddenly the hobbling man is inside a house. He suddenly swings the axe in a wide arc over his head and brings it crashing down onto a white door, splintering the wood into pieces.

The sound of a woman sobbing. She might be behind the splintered door. Suddenly he is scared out of his wits.

Dad looks up from the paper, puts a finger to his mouth, licks it and then turns a page.

But, perhaps he's got this all wrong. It's very confusing. He doesn't understand. It's adult stuff. Because in the next scene there's a man in an interview and then a family is in a car - boy, mum, dad all close together. The creepy music's stopped. But there's something about the man's grinning face that he really doesn't like. Something about those eyes and the high, dark eyebrows. The smile looks crazy and the eyes somehow cruel.

—

There's the little boy, about his age, maybe younger, eating some bread and drinking milk with his mum at the table. So, things are okay now. He can relax, perhaps. He realises he has been holding his breath. But still something is not quite right. Noise creeping in the background, low and unsettling, like something quiet and predatory. He almost spits out his biscuit when suddenly the little boy's face fills the screen and his eyes pop and his mouth contorts into a scream. The screen flickers with strobe lighting. He looks away. He really doesn't want to see any more of this.

'What is this?' Dad looks up from behind his paper.

He cannot help seeing this. He'd turn it off, but dad always has the TV controller. He lifts his hands to his face and watches through his fingers. His heart is pounding. If he could, he'd look away, but he just can't look away.

The little boy is riding a tricycle. Peddling as fast as he can down a long line of dark bushes. It is dark and snowy, probably very late at night. Is there a moon creating this ominously pale light? The boy seems to be in some kind of maze. Desperately he wants this little boy to go faster, to hurry, hurry, faster, faster. Now the crazy man is in the maze. Lurching along, panting like a dog, eyes rolling with craziness. He is carrying the big axe, low slung, between his hands, just above the knees. The look on his face is demented - the boy is sure he must be what is called a maniac. The maniac might be chasing the boy and is going to cut him to pieces, chop him up with the big axe. He doesn't know why. He can't imagine why. It is so horrible.

'What is this? I don't think you should be watching this,' dad says and suddenly switches the channels.

So he doesn't see how it ends.

But that night and every night for a week or more he sees the shadow of the man, lumbering across the snow, with his axe carried, slung low, like a weapon, chasing a small boy who cannot go fast enough, frantically peddling his trike, faster, faster, faster.

But not fast enough.

2

They were worried about the hands. The rest of the bodies were not much different from the other children's drawings. Big heads, scratched-in hair, stick bodies and limbs, big, zig-zagging smiles across round faces. Lop-sided, sticky out ears. And up above the figures, often the sun in orange or yellow. A circle surrounded by lines.

But the hands on the figures were not just a series of twigs, like on the other children's pictures. These are big hands, detailed hands, with fingers and a thumb. Yes, okay, perhaps that might suggest artistic talent, but what has really worried them is that these hands are uniformly, on every figure and on every one of his drawings, black. That's why they've called his mother into school and are whispering to her about him while he waits outside the classroom door, anxiously listening.

3

The face seemed ordinary enough. Black and more grey than white, the texture is grainy, like it has been damaged, stained somehow. Perhaps it is an old photo, perhaps the only one they could find. A snapshot that might be kept in a wallet.

11

An unremarkable face stares out, directly eyeing the viewer. The eyes don't shy away or avoid the lens. Dark, deep-set eyes, but not obviously hostile. The eyebrows thick, the nose a bit squidgy. An awful lot of very dark, fuzzy hair.

The face might be smiling, a little - the mouth is open, slightly ajar. There is a small gap in the middle of the top teeth. Small white teeth, sitting neatly enough in a row. A thin top lip. Conceivably the face might even be expressing happiness.

Black facial hair too - a moustache, with beard, cut a bit like a Spanish nobleman. The pale face speckled with grey dots and blotches and enclosed entirely by a fuzz of darkness.

After seeing it on TV, on the nine o'clock news, he cannot get the face out of his head. Nor that word - 'ripper'. Not for weeks nor months. Not for years.

4

He doesn't quite know what the word 'dismembered' means. But he knows enough to know he doesn't like the sound of it. He doesn't like it at all. But, still, he decides he has to find out. Afterwards he files it with other taboo words - 'sexual abuse', 'abduction', 'maniac', 'ripper'.

5.

The man in the yellow capri is smiling. The car window is open and the man is resting his elbow on the door, leaning out a little from the car and smiling, smiling at him. Long, thick sideburns, dark raggedy hair and a pale, slightly sweaty complexion. He might be about thirty, though it's hard to be sure.

Smiling, the man tells him that his mother is not able to pick him up from school and she has asked him to do so instead, as a favour. Hop in and he'll run him straight home. It's no bother. His capri is sporty, with spoilers and fancy alloy wheels.

Not Forgotten

With her fine, expensive-looking clothes, haughty manner and cut-glass voice, Great Aunty May was a very grand lady indeed. She'd come over on the boat all the way from Canada where she lived in apparently great style with a wealthy husband who was something big in mining and she would be visiting their humble little abode only briefly, she informed them, during a whistle stop tour of the old country. Her opulent lifestyle must be a stark contrast indeed to their own life of grim and grinding poverty and the children sensed their mother's awkward self-consciousness in front of this impossibly regal relative, who, with her fine blue dress and extravagantly feathered hat seemed altogether too big for and altogether out-of-place in the cramped kitchen of their humble two-up, two-down end of terrace. Now she was standing by the window, delicately sipping from a cup of tea and looking around her with barely concealed distaste.

Since father had died on the rail tracks, things have been tougher than ever for mother. There was the shame of father's death, of course, they all felt that keenly, along with the terrible sadness, and none so more than mother. More immediately pressing though was the problem of making increasingly tattered ends meet. Fortunately Aunty Ellen lived up the road and could look after the four little urchins, Agnes, the eldest, Bunny, Nessie and the youngest, Jack, when mother went out in the evenings to scrub the floors of the local pubs. This after a full day's work at home or slaving in the shop. Aunty Ellen had never married and had no children of her own. You couldn't call Aunty Ellen warm, exactly, but she was down-to-earth and had, so mother said, her head screwed on right. Over time, the children had grown used to her rather dour ways.

But none of them could ever have imagined, even in their wildest dreams, that they might be related to someone as grand and imposing as this elegant figure, a proper society lady, someone who wouldn't be out of place, perhaps, taking tea with the King and the rest of the royal family.

From what she could glean of the adults' sometimes hushed conversation, Great Aunty May, it seemed, had something called a 'proposal' to which her mother appeared to be listening with great attention and keen, bright-eyed interest.

✳

Less than a decade after that fateful visit and Agnes was now nearly fourteen and had spent a whole year working tirelessly up at the grand hall, Upton House, as a tweeny, a small part of the domestic staff in the employ of Lord and Lady Hartnell. Mostly her work involved getting up at the crack of dawn, before anyone else in the household was up, and lighting the various fires in various rooms, the kitchen, the scullery, the sitting room and so forth. Then the rest of the day would be spent washing, scrubbing and scouring or sweeping, dusting and polishing everything in sight and even some things out of sight until the whole place and every object within it was spotlessly clean. For wasn't cleanliness next to Godliness, as Mrs. Banks so liked to remind her. Anything less than impeccable and Mrs. Banks would be on her case and she'd have to clean everything again, from the start, as punishment for slackness.

On top of all this she was often put to work like a slave in the kitchen, helping cook to prepare lavish breakfasts, lunches and dinners and then clearing up all the mess afterwards. Then there was the fetching and carrying and the general ad hoc chores and the errands and always, all the time, being told by everybody, old and young, above and below stairs, what she must do and having to smile back and curtesy and appear at all times to be meek and ever so grateful, thank you so very much.

It was dull, repetitive, physically exhausting work, hard on the hands, harder on her knees, and seemingly endless. Seven days a week, with only Sunday mornings off to attend church and, if she performed her duties to the sharp-eyed satisfaction of Mrs. Banks, a whole precious day off once a fortnight.

For all this miserable drudgery she was paid a pittance and, even among the servants, with whom she was only permitted to eat on special occasions, she was right at the very bottom of the pile. If she ever, for one moment, forgot her place, she was quickly and firmly reminded of it, sometimes painfully. She hated this existence, for that was all it was, an existence, with all the great passion of her heart. But, she knew too, she must be thankful for it – for didn't she have stable employment as well as a place to live, albeit a small, narrow, dingy room with a single bed at the top of a creaky old staircase.

Mother had cried that first day when they'd said goodbye and Agnes had promised her she'd write home at least once a week and, if she managed to save the odd penny or two, that, yes, she'd send this too with the letters. And dutifully she had done so for almost a whole year, always downplaying in her letters the misery and always putting a shiny gloss on any small mercies or acts of kindness that might on rare occasions come her way.

When still no letter had come after a fortnight, mother became

---

increasingly fretful and when four long weeks had passed and there was still no word from Agnes, she was beside herself with the worry. There was nothing for it, then, she'd leave the other three children with her sister, Ellen, and walk the ten miles or so to Upton Hall and find out what had happened to her eldest daughter.

And so it was that mother had found herself now standing by the back entrance to the grandest house she had ever clapped eyes upon, nervously waiting for someone to answer her timid knocking.

A bald, sour-faced man in what she took to be a butler's uniform stood at the doorway and looked down his long nose at her.

'Yes, what do you want?' The tone certainly wasn't friendly.

She'd asked him had he seen her daughter, Agnes? She was employed at the Hall as a tweeny. Had been so for a year or so. Usually she wrote home once a week, she explained, but they'd heard nothing for almost a month now and so she was sick with worry.

The man listened impatiently and arched an eyebrow. 'Agnes?' he said, 'Oh yes, we know Agnes all right. But she's not here. She disappeared one morning. When would it be? Perhaps a fortnight ago.'

O her poor heart. Did she leave a note or anything to say where she might be heading?

'Oh yes,' the bald man scowled at her. 'She left a note, of sorts, in the dust on a sideboard in the parlour she'd left scandalously unclean for days, scrawled with a finger. 'Gone,' it said, 'but not forgotten'.'

✳

———

17

Here they were among the crowds milling at the docks - Great Aunty May in her long elegant coat with the fox fur trimmings and her hat with the feathers, and mother too in her Sunday best, her one plain, smart dress, and herself, Agnes, and little Nessie in their school pinnies, come to say their fond farewells. The two boys had already said tearful goodbyes and were at home being looked after by Aunty Ellen.

Great Aunty May was checking the tickets and making sure they joined the right queue for the ship that would take them off across half the world. Agnes was old enough to realise mother was trying hard to hold back tears. She clutched their little hands firmly as their Great Aunt led them implacably towards the departure gates.

Of course, it was sweet little, gentle little, cute little Nessie who had been chosen to accompany her Great Aunt. Little Nessie who had been granted this miraculous chance to start a whole new, far, far better life on the other side of the world, in Canada.

They were nearly there now. They could see the great white ship, docked in the harbour and the people with their suitcases and bags and belongings crowding around. Little Nessie clutching a small bag in one hand and her mother's hand in the other.

And then, it seemed, mother couldn't stand it any longer. They were going to have to say their goodbyes right now, because, oh heart, she really couldn't bear it a moment longer.

'As you wish,' said Great Aunty May, taking Nessie firmly by the hand. 'You know, it's the right thing to do. I promise you we shall look after her as if she were our ownl.'

Mother looked as if her heart was about to burst.

'Wait,' she said desperately. 'Wait, please, May. Please, I've changed my mind.'

＊

Via a long, apologetic letter, they learnt a while later, to their great relief, that somehow, despite sending a regular lifeline of pennies home to support her mother and younger siblings, Agnes had managed to squirrel away enough of her paltry pay to save up and buy a one-way train ticket to London. She was barely fourteen years old, but was settled now in the Great Smoke and had managed to find a nice place to live and had secured a good job, working, she said, on the buses.

＊

Many, many years later Agnes would marry a soldier and move all the way to Karachi. But her whole, long life she'd never forget that moment at the docks in Liverpool, with mother, Nessie and Great Aunty May.

＊

'Wait! Stop, please. Sorry, but I've changed my mind.'

And then, the long held back tears had come freely and she had grabbed little Nessie's hand and pulled her away from Great Aunty May and clasped into her own tender embrace, her whole body rising and falling with the violence of the sobbing, Nessie nestled gratefully into her mother's midriff and hugged her back with all her small might.

19

And when Agnes had looked up at Great Aunty May she could see the shock too in that grand, haughty face. Mixed, perhaps with anger or distaste. Her long, slender arms were folded across her chest, her thin lips were pursed and she was staring disapprovingly at her poor, foolish, sentimental niece.

There was a shrill whistle and then a man in a smart uniform was shouting that it was time for them to go through the barriers and to start boarding the huge white ship.

'So be it,' said Great Aunty May breezily, 'it's your choice, however foolhardy. I fear you shall both live to regret it. But there we are.' She tutted and picked up her travelling bag. 'You do understand that I offered that girl an opportunity the like of which you can scarcely even begin to imagine.'

And then her mother had looked up at her grand aunt, brushed the tears away from her eyes and spoken those words.

'Would you take her, instead?' she'd said, pointing. 'Would you take Agnes?'

As long as she lived, Agnes could never erase them, those few, confusing, scalding words from her mind, nor forget how they had brought her heart rushing up and almost out of her mouth and the blood come flushing to her cheeks.

Great Aunt May turned and looked down at the other child. It was as if she was seeing this odd little girl properly for the first time. There was a coolly appraising look in her pale blue eyes. From what she'd seen and heard, this child was far less sweet-natured and biddable and was certainly not as attractive looking as her angelic younger sister. There was a definite look of defiance about this one, a hardness in the eyes, a tightness about her mouth, the raised chin.

Above Agnes, in the dizzyingly blue air, seagulls went screeching past. Around her, the bustle and clamour of the crowd, now surging forward. And then the huge ship blowing its long, mournful whistle and the sunlight hitting the water hard and erupting into stars.

And finally her great aunt's voice cutting through everything, like a blade, clear and distinct: 'This one?' she said as she began to move away, 'No, I don't think so, thank you very much. This one can stay here with you.'

Stop in the Name of Love

Seventeen-year-old girls were wondrous goddesses. Like movie stars, they lived their lives in full dazzling technicolour with complimentary wrap-around sound and attendant trails of heady, intoxicating perfume. Independent, mysterious, daring creatures, they lived liberated lives, lives full of unimaginable adventure. Coming and going from home with their own set of front door keys and at times of their own choosing, some of these miraculous beings even travelled under their own steam. Some drove cars, others had boyfriends with their own garishly coloured cars, boyfriends who sometimes featured sprouts of manly facial hair. To him, seventeen-year-old girls were glossy, new-minted adults, glistening with a sheen of sophistication. Vibrantly alive, they radiated exotic allure. Though these goddesses might be adults, they were of an entirely different species to the tired and worn, boring common-or-garden varieties of adults he came across every day - parents and teachers and relations and that sort of tired old thing.

Of course, seventeen-year-old goddesses paid no attention to little squits like him. Despite their dreamy obsessions and fervent adorations, second year boys were virtually invisible to seventeen-year-old girls, of little more interest to them than the pavement they seemed to glide across. But a seventeen-year girl's smile had a super-power, like Superman's eyes. If one of those smiles hit you, it could send your heart thudding so hard you feared all your mates must be able to hear it. The slightest touch of one of those electric smiles beamed at you, for even a second, could send colour rushing unbidden to your cheeks and make your knees knock together.

Paul's older sister, the almost adult, glorious goddess was, he had learnt, named Jasmin. Jasmin - even her name was like an enchanting exotic breeze. Jasmin, like a beautiful princess in the Arabian Nights. He'd seen Jasmin a couple of times dropping Paul off at school, in her own car. But it was not exotic, near-adult Jasmin who'd written him the letter, his first ever letter from a teenage girl. No, it was the middle sister, Emma, who must have been no more that fourteen and, he remembered ruefully, rather plain and plump.

Generally speaking, up until his new-found infatuation with older women, he hadn't been much interested in girls per se, certainly not ones around his own age, no, not really. Attending an all-boys school, he didn't happen across girls much in the general course of things and anyway he was more interested in healthily boyish pursuits - football, cricket, The Lord of the Rings, super-hero comics and, lately, computer games. At his mixed primary school, they'd played kiss-chase, but since then, girls weren't really on his radar.

When he'd been to Paul's house for tea, he had hardly even noticed the middle sister. Not said more than a gruff 'hello' to her. It was his first time at Paul's and once he'd discovered that Jasmin wasn't going to be around, he was too preoccupied by his new friend's empire to notice much else. Particularly spectacular was Paul's bedroom. With the flourish of a matador, Paul had pulled open a desk drawer to reveal a veritable treasure trove of treats - heaps of chocolate bars – proper ones - Mars Bars, Marathons, Twixes - plus assorted bags of sweets, soft sweets, boiled sweets, fruit flavours and mints, caramels and toffees – a whole drawerful, in fact, of impossibly sumptuous delights.

When they'd arrived at Paul's place, after school, Paul's mum had given them a whole chocolate bar and a can of real coke, not the cheaper supermarket stuff he had, sometimes, as a treat at home. This had been

———

the first sign of the wonders to come. But not in his greediest dreams had he imagined such a drawerful of deliciousness from which, like a sultan, Paul could pluck one delicacy after another when and wherever he felt inclined, without need of any permission at all from a superior authority.

Unfettered access to sweets and chocolate turned out, however, to be the least of the marvels of Paul's bedroom. A pristine Subbuteo pitch was laid out on a hard board tabletop. A perfect fit and smooth as an ironed shirt. Not a single kink disturbed the crisp, taut, bottle-green fabric. Clearly, unlike his own inferior version, this pitch didn't have to be put away between games. What was more, Paul's was the latest, top-notch set, the sublime international edition, with nets on the goalposts, corner flags and even a dug out for the manager and trainer.

But even that wonder was made to seem a dull commonplace when set against the magnificence of the object sitting on a desk in the corner of the bedroom, a brand-spanking new computer! Not only that but, oh holy of holies, a ZX Spectrum, no less. Every boy in his class desperately wanted a ZX Spectrum. It was top of every birthday list and every Christmas list. He'd tried rolling birthday and Christmas into one big present, without any luck and, as far as he knew, Paul was the only boy in his class who actually owned one of these divine dream machines.

At home they had a sad old Atari, strictly yesterday's tech. Its bulky console could be attached to the TV and on in one could play, at best, Pong, if the thing was actually working. Now Paul was showing off his well-honed skills on the ZX Spectrum. Impatiently he awaited his turn. And then it was with trembling fingers and with a quivering heart, like an acolyte before the holy altar, that he had held that beautifully designed joystick and played his first games of Astro-Blaster, Defender and then best of all, Barbarian. This ZX Spectrum was a super-computer. Its graphics were out of this world!

Even when mum'd picked him up from Paul's and driven him home, his head was still giddy with all the glories of his new best friend's house. And it was only as he was taking off his coat, when he'd got home, that he noticed something odd, stuffed into one its pockets.

A small bundle of paper, lilac-coloured, tied carefully with a purple satin bow. Some instinct made him hide it in his trousers before anyone else saw it. How could this mysterious, alien object have gotten into the pocket of his coat? There was something definitely feminine about it, so he didn't think it could have been from Paul. Certainly he hoped not.

Fortunately, he had had enough sense to take the bundle up to his bedroom before untying it and reading in private. Curiously the bundle had a vaguely flowery scent, like the smell of the dried flowers in the bowl mum put in the lavatory. He opened it up and realised immediately that it was a letter.

After hurriedly reading the letter through a couple of times and blushing a little at the mention of his sexy deep voice, beautiful blue eyes and broad, manly shoulders, he tried to think of somewhere safe he could stash it. Maybe, he thought, it would be better if to destroy it. He could stuff the letter into the bottom of the kitchen bin perhaps or burn it in the garden. But it'd be hard to do either without some risk of discovery. And, besides, his vanity meant that he really kind of wanted to keep the letter. He read through its contents for a third time. Manly shoulders, that was good, surely.

Finally, he decided his best bet was to tuck into the bottom his wardrobe, in his secret place, near his small collection of photos of semi-naked women he'd culled furtively from his parents' Sunday magazines and one from mum's clothes catalogues. That would be the safest place for it. Nobody was likely to rummage around and find it in there.

A few days later and they were all sitting at the dining room table about to eat dinner. His kid sister and older brother and he were waiting for mum to bring in the food and arguing, as usual, about who'd had to lay the table and whose turn it would be to clear away afterwards. As usual, dad was still at work. When mum came in from the kitchen, carrying a casserole dish, she had a huge smile on her face.

'Before we eat, I found some very interesting reading material today,' she said in a breezy manner and she put down the dish and took her place at the head of the table, 'which I thought I might share over dinner...'

Oh my God. It couldn't be. If so, that meant... Oh my God. No.

'Or perhaps, Michael,' she smiled warmly at him, 'you'd care to read it to us, and here I am quoting directly, in your 'deep manly, sexy voice...'

Then and there, as he listened to the interminable words and his mother's accompanying laugher, he vowed that he would never, ever give his heart away in love.

Choking on a Fly

I don't want to talk about it. You're upsetting me now. What good can it do? Opening up these old wounds?

You can't have heard the warning, the anger in his voice, because, for some reason, you just wouldn't go to bed. Which really wasn't like you, to be disobedient like that.

I hadn't a chance to react, I didn't really know what was happening. I froze, I think - I just couldn't think or move fast enough. What could I have done anyway? Realistically. It really did all happen in such a blur, so fast. Too fast. I think probably I shouted out something. Honestly, I can't remember. I know I jumped up from where I was sitting.

That sudden fury, that sudden rage just as suddenly just went out of him. I was shouting and up on my feet by then too and your brother had got hold of him. I think the red mist just cleared suddenly and then all the anger just as suddenly went out of him.

Survival instinct I suppose, trying to protect your stomach and your head.

Afterwards, when it was over, I took you upstairs. You were shaking badly and terribly upset - crying, shaking, couldn't catch your breath, wet all over. I hugged you close, comforted and calmed you down. A few puffs on your inhaler helped get your breathing under control and then you had a shower or perhaps it was a bath. I don't remember.

Yes, that's right, Abba, was it, on our smart new record player, in the corner of the lounge. Both of us, we really liked singing along to 'Waterloo' and 'Dancing Queen' especially. We'd be singing along like crazy, hairbrushes for mikes, dancing around each other, pretending we were on 'Top of the Pops' or something crazy and we were just having such a good time.

No, you were good, most of the time. We couldn't complain, really. Not rude, like some the kids nowadays. Not like that friend of yours, that cocky one. Sometimes you tried to be funny though, making wisecracks, always sailing a little too close to the wind.

He was across the room in the blink of an eye. I'd never seen him so angry or move so fast. I think he might have had a drink or two to be honest with you. He did like a drink. To be honest, I think they both did.

Yes, we wanted to have a few more dances, that was all. I just, I just didn't see it coming. I'd never seen him like that ever before. Haven't ever since. And that's God's honest truth. Trust me, I'm telling you that.

Yes, nearly six foot and those days, probably around fifteen stone or thereabouts. Yes, I suppose, a powerful man, you could say that. And, yes, only a boy. Maybe nine or ten, eleven at most. It all happened so many years ago, it's hard to remember it all precisely, the details. I suppose, over the years, I've sort of blotted it out. It was so out of.... He just wasn't like that, normally.

You just sort of collapsed in a heap, on the carpet. Curled up. Like a baby.

You have to understand the context. I'm not saying it excuses anything.

The irony was, you two were so much alike.

No, not really. Not enough to justify, anything like that. What would? That was partly why it was such a shock. It seemed to come completely out of the blue. He just snapped. Lost his rag. No, absolutely not. Never. He wasn't, isn't, you know, not at all and he hadn't been drinking. We didn't, not in those days. It wasn't late. I suppose, we may have been firm with you children, at times, by modern standards, but that was called disciplined in our day.

Yes, it's true, he did have a bit of a temper on him, sometimes, who doesn't? A short fuse, yes. But it was all over and done with pretty quickly. I don't think you were really hurt, were you, just shaken up a bit.

We never hurt any of you, never would, not in a million years. You know that. And, never again, either. I wouldn't have stood for it. It just really wasn't like him.

You'd have been about seven or eight, would you, I think.

He allowed himself to be pulled away as he suddenly realised, I think, what he was doing. It was all over in, it can't have been more than, maybe, a few seconds, not much more. But it wasn't like him, really it wasn't, you know that. It was all such a long, long time ago.

There was a lot of pressure, at work, huge pressure. The recent promotion, the senior management job he'd been given, finally after a long struggle to prove himself at that bloody company. It was a big company too and he was responsible for a lot of people's jobs and the company was going through a really rough time, financially and not because of him, of any decisions he'd made, but bad ones, ones they'd inherited and had to deal with.

I don't think, in the end, he actually even touched you, did he? Just a lot of shouting. Hot air. No real damage done. You'd said something, some smart-arse comment or other, had you? Probably, knowing you.

The whole economy, it was in a really bad shape and getting worse by the day, it seemed. Things were difficult. He had a lot on his plate. I'm not making excuses, I'm really not, but, on top of all that, my father was ill, terminally ill it turned out. So, all told, we were all under a lot of strain.

I was very young, maybe only six or seven. We were just singing and dancing. I must have shut my eyes, I think.

You two liked to dance sometimes after dinner, in the kitchen. You'd put on the radio and you'd dance. I remember you particularly liked a collection of songs from the film 'Grease' - 'You're the One that I Want', 'Grease Lightning' - that sort of thing. He'd be reading the paper, I'd be tidying up after dinner. You two'd singalong, doing all the actions, like John Travolta, wiggling around. It made us all laugh. You were pretty good. But then you just wouldn't go to bed when you were told to. It wasn't like you to be so openly defiant.

Sorry, but I didn't see. Possibly I didn't want to see. I don't remember seeing. But I did hear, some of it, even though I put my hands over my ears and the music was still playing. The shouting. I remember that. And a little later, you, crying.

He was up from the table like a shot. I hadn't seen him move so fast in a very long time. Hurled down his paper and just lost it. In a few seconds he must have been halfway across the lounge and it was quite a large room.

You had a look on your face, I'll never forget it, a look of sheer shock, I think.

And absolute terror.

I told you to come downstairs once you'd cleaned himself up and put on your p-jays and dressing gown. At the time I thought that was important - to broker some sort of a reconciliation. He was in his study, working on some papers, as usual. I made you two apologise.

Curled yourself up, like a baby, hands tight over your head.

Okay, I made you apologise to him, for being so cheeky, and asked you to give him a hug, which, reluctantly, you did. Maybe I wasn't thinking entirely straight and that, that, perhaps wasn't the right thing to do, yes, I think so, now.

Once the kids were in bed, I want you to know, we had a blazing row that evening.

I heard shouting, something really loud. Roaring and swearing. And then my older brother was shouting and then I heard mum shouting too. Suddenly everyone seemed to be screaming and shouting and moving in all directions quickly. When I opened my eyes you were on the floor, curled up.

That's when I dashed over and somehow managed to pull him away before it was too late.

You're upsetting me now.

Really I don't want to talk about it.
What good can it possibly do, opening up these old wounds?

Perhaps it's for me.

Straight Bat

Among themselves, all the boys called him 'Bendy', though his official teacher title was Mr. Croft. They called him 'Bendy' simply because that was what the older boys called him and naturally they followed their elders' lead. They didn't know why Mr. Croft was always 'Bendy'. At least, not really, not at first.

Bendy Croft was head of P.E. at their school. A notorious bully, quick with sarky putdowns that made his favourite boys snigger complicitly, he was an old-fashioned type of P.E. teacher. The sort who wouldn't be allowed anywhere near small children these days. When, for instance, it was snowing or hailing or sleeting and the weather was so bad it was impossible to play rugby or football and the boys were sent off to slog around muddy, saturated fields in the freezing cold, Bendy Croft would stand in the middle of the playing fields, dressed in so many layers he looked like a Michelin man, shouting the odd word of encouragement at the frontrunners or perhaps some well-chosen disparagement ridiculing the fat and/or weedy kids lagging at the back, his gloved hands cupped around a nice hot mug of tea. Rarely had any of the boys seen Bendy Croft break out into a run.

Bendy Croft could be cruel, malicious, vindictive, even, yes the word's not too strong, sadistic. No boy wanted to get the wrong, nasty side of Bendy Croft, especially if they were good at sport and wanted to make the school or county team.

Onetime, Bendy Croft knocked fatty Binks clean off his feet playing murderball in the old gym. Murderball seemed to be a game Bendy

---

Croft had invented and one he particularly delighted in playing. Murderball involved the class of first year boys in their white vests and shorts running barefoot in a circle around their teacher. Round and round they ran across the slippery floor of the school gym. In the centre of their circle stood Bendy Croft posed with a medicine ball held above his head. Without warning their teacher would take aim and hurl the ball at any one of the boys skittering past. That ball was heavy. But also hard to throw very fast. And the boys were mostly nimble-footed and, in any case, there was some distance between them and their teacher. Nearly all the time, the boys were easily quick enough to avoid the sluggish ball. If it did hit you, usually it was only a glancing blow. Then you were out and watched the rest of the game from the wooded benches. But Fatty Binks wasn't quick. Nor was he nimble.

There'd been a sickening crack as Fatty Binks' soft head had hit the hard wood. And then, also, shockingly, blood. As Bendy Croft knelt beside the stricken figure, he had sent another boy to run-off and to quick, fetch the school nurse, while the others were hurried away to get changed ready for their next lesson. In the end, Fatty Binks survived the ordeal with just a bit of bruising, a cut and some hurt pride to show for his trouble. But that was the last time anyone played Murderball at our school.

Bendy Croft who was an old boy and had never taught at any other school. Bendy Croft who, they said, could have made it as a professional goalkeeper if he'd hadn't been so terribly short. Bendy Croft who each year arranged for the second-year football team to go on a school tour, with him as the only accompanying adult. Bendy Croft who curried favour with the football boys by taking them to see movies their parents would never have allowed them to see. Bendy Croft who told them that if they forgot their swimming trunks they'd have to swim naked in the school's unheated outdoor pool. Bendy Croft who

---

watched avidly from the hatch as the boys took their communal showers. Whereas all the other P.E. teachers asked one of the boys to hand out the small, rough towels to the others once they'd run through the dribbly showers, Bendy Croft always kept that job for himself.

Bendy Croft who selected the boys to go forward for the district and county teams for football and cricket and once invited a scout from a first division team to work with the football squad. Bendy Croft who'd told his parents that he was an unusually talented cricketer and that he played the cover drive with the straightest bat he'd ever seen for a boy in the first year. Despite, or perhaps because of this, he'd never been one of Bendy Croft's favourites, thank God.

What did the other teachers think of their colleague? Who knew? The lives of teachers were entirely mysterious to the boys. But from what they could tell, Bendy Croft got along perfectly well with his colleagues at school. Did they know what the boys openly called him?

When one of the boys was injured in a football match, it was Bendy Croft who'd run on, of course, in his tight blue adidas tracksuit, a bucket of cold water and sponge in hand to tend lovingly to the wound. Bendy Croft's hands would run over the youthful skin, checking for any tenderness and sometimes a boy might have to emphasise that the injury was lower down, nearer to the knee, Sir.

Many years later, long after he had left school, been through university, got married, had his own children, moved away to another town, his mother had shown him the article on the front pages of the local newspaper. Mr. Croft had been arrested, charged and found guilty of a series of sex crimes against boys committed over a number of years. Bendy Croft would serve many years in prison.

'I could never put my finger on it exactly,' his mother had said as she hovered over the article, 'but I always felt there was something not quite right about that man.'

Fleabag

That's what we called him, what all the children called him at their primary school, Fleabag. One of the gypsy lads who lived at the far end, on the outskirts of their village, near the straggly woods and down the pot-holed lane that no respectable folk would ever want to visit, especially at night. Gipsy Lane, in fact. It was where all the local gypsies lived and ran scrap metal businesses, their yards piled with metal junk, guarded by large, fierce dogs. Their children came to the local primary school, sometimes: Big Jimmy Ginger, as large as a bus and as slow; nasty Micky Rivers who once put dog shit in another kid's school lunch bag just for laughs; a small, runty kid who collected bogies in his wooden desk, and then there was good old Fleabag.

Fleabag's dad, they overheard their parents telling each other in conspiratorial, disapproving voices, never worked, had, in fact, never done an honest day's work in his entire good-for-nothing life. He was a shameless layabout, a sponger on the state, a parasite, a ne'er-do-well. Rumours said he got drunk every night and lay in bed all day, while his raggedy children went to school and his wife to work cleaning the poshest local houses. He was on the state and not, scandalously, apparently ashamed of it at all. It was suspected too that he has a short, scratchy temper and a free way with his large fists.

In the evenings Fleabag's mum sold the football pools. She'd come round their well-to-do middle-class estates, slowly pedalling her old-fashioned, rickety bicycle, the tyres wheezing asthmatically as she went. She'd knock on doors to see did anyone want the chance of getting rich on the pools. When they knew it was her, the children didn't want to answer the door to find her standing on their doorsteps

---

half-lit by the porch light. They knew it was unkind, but with her hairy warts, motheaten coat and crumpled hat and her old-fashioned bike, she looked like the wicked witch of the west, and in their hearts, they feared she might read their thoughts and curse them with her gypsy eye or perhaps, so the littlest feared, kidnap them and roast them over a gypsy campfire for her tea.

Their mothers would scold them, tell them that this was just a poor old woman, utterly harmless, and how ashamed they should be of theirselves with their silly, cruel stories. They should just get the door next time the bell rang and be polite and quick about it. Or else there'd be trouble. Their mothers would always dutifully buy a coupon and have a quick chat on the front doorstep, though, to their relief, the front doors were always kept only half-open and Mrs. Fleabag was never invited inside any of their neat, well-furnished houses.

It was a combination of his looks and the smell, that's how he got the name, probably. No-one remembered choosing it for him, or using it for the first time. But it stuck like mud. It was just naturally what everyone called him. His hair was dull, coarse and mousey-coloured. The cruellest children compared it to a toilet brush. Home cut, no doubt, with a bowl and a rough pair of scissors. Underneath this thatch his face was oddly foreign-looking – perhaps Mongolian; almond-shaped and flat-featured, with sallow, greyish skin. But it was the eyes especially give him his strange, foreign look - brown, gentle, docile and slanted, they thought, like a chinaman's. What the children called, unflatteringly, his slitty eyes.

Then there was the smell, the strong, musty smell that came off him. Because, truth be told, Fleabag didn't wash much. Or perhaps, more accurately, he wasn't washed much. His large hands and defenceless, open face always looked grubby and his stale-smelling clothes were old-fashioned, hand-me-downs, none of them quite fitting. Tired off-white shirt, jumpers with holes in the elbows, too short grey trousers with straggly cuffs. Never any socks above a pair of scuffed, out-sized old-man's brown brogues. Mind, no-one washed as much in those days; even respectable children had bath nights only at the weekend and showers were a rare modern luxury. But Fleabag looked like he hadn't seen a sponge, let alone a bath, in a long time. Smelly was the word that sprung all too easily to their minds and mouths. All the kids said he had fleas.

A goofy, good-hearted, lopsided grin and stuttering, nervous laugh, which, as he got the joke, built to a hearty guffawing explosion of sound. There was an old-world, unkempt, free-wheeling, untamed quality about him. A country lad, if he could have sucked on a straw while sitting on a gate to watch the world go by, he probably would have done. In olden times, he might have been called a bumpkin or an oaf or a simpleton. His other life, outside of school, was mysteriously alien to them. He was the sort of boy who might keep half-eaten apples or even baby birds or ferrets in his capacious pockets. He might be tender-hearted towards small, injured creatures he found in fields, nursing them painstakingly back to health to release them secretly into the wild. He might spend his nights poaching game from the local estate or perhaps fishing barefoot by moonlight in the local streams.

But school was always a terrible, humiliating struggle. Not very good at his sums, a slow, hesitant reader, shy and awkward in class, somehow clumsily out of place, he suffered his role of class dunce with seeming good humour. What other choice did he have?

That name he carried from primary to secondary school like a leper's bell. At the big school they hardly saw him for a while. Inevitably he was in the bottom set, 'F', for failure, for everything and, except at sports, top and bottom sets, like soap and Fleabag, never mixed. Then, briefly, they were friends again in the third year. Generously, they took him under their wing for a while. An act of conscious charity, of pity perhaps. They just sort of felt sorry for him and they knew he had a good ticker, old Fleabag.

One time they took him to a school disco together in their car. Dressed in his finest, a jacket and tie no less, after-shaved, that coarse hair brylcreemed. Like a proper old-fashioned gent. And he was so grateful for such small acts of friendship and respect.

But, all too soon, he became a pain, so needy, a hanger-on, an unwelcome guest, turning up at every corner, sticking to them, like mud. They knew in their hearts that their friendship was patronizing. Really they had so very little in common. And so quietly, they withdrew, avoided bumping into him at school during lunch and break times, took different routes home, stopped inviting him into their games, dropped him as gently but firmly as they could as a friend. If he resented it, he never said anything, never complained. Good old Fleabag.

After school, naturally, they went their separate ways. They headed off to university and, so they heard, he joined the army, infantry, of course.

Last time they saw old Fleabag, he was striding down the street of their local village towards them. They'd felt obliged to stop briefly for a cursory chat. How was he? How were things? They'd been away at Uni and here he was kitted out head-to-foot in splendid army green. The smartest they'd ever seen him – red beret worn at a jaunty angle, perfectly polished black boots. Back straight, chest out, big smile, proud as a rooster. A proper grown-up man, while they were still just boys playing at life. He hadn't lost that shy, goofy smile, nor the big, slow-building, guffawing laugh. Nor the same meek gratitude for them deigning to be friendly to one as lowly as him.

Much later, they heard that I was killed in the first gulf war.

The Coldness, 1

She was a council estate girl, unlike the rest of this group of friends. Though later she'd realise they were hardly posh, to her nine-year-old self, these friends seemed to come from a higher echelon of society than her. They all lived in bigger houses, houses on wider, tree-lined streets, houses not crammed into a single estate. Homes their parents owned. Not council houses or an estate. Some of her friends' houses were detached and they were all different shapes and sizes.

Plus these children just had more stuff and better, newer stuff than her. Though it was beautifully made by mother's deft hands, her summer dress was not bought from shops, like Susan's dresses were. She was aware of that, but really she didn't mind. She'd admit she was envious, though, of her friends' bikes, especially her best friend Anne's brand new one. Because a bike opened up and expanded the world. She might not be much interested in the speed you could go, unlike the boys, but the fact that you could go so much further on a bike, the freedom a bike afforded, that's what attracted her. As Anne told anyone and everyone who'd listen, she had been given her brand-new bike for her birthday by her father and it was still so nearly new its brightly coloured chrome was shiny from the shop.

Not that she was ashamed or embarrassed about what she didn't have or where she lived, not at all. It may have been only a council estate, but it wasn't a rough place, despite what some people said. It wasn't rundown in the way she already knew some council estates could be. Built not long before the war, her council estate was well kept. Moreover, it was a friendly, safe place to grow-up. Nearly everybody knew everybody else and mother and father always said it had a good, strong, solid sense of community.

Her friends' houses may have been grander, but mother and father took great pride in their own home and always kept the house and its small garden ship-shape and in neat working order. Father was skilled with his hands and ensured that the front door and window frames were regularly sanded and painted, the front gate regularly varnished and oiled and the small lawn mown regularly at the weekends in the summer while mother made sure the beds were neatly tended with colourful flowers and shrubs. Cleanliness may have been closest to Godliness, but, in her house, tidiness ran it a close second.

Despite their greater affluence, she didn't feel inferior to her posher friends not really. For one thing she was a bright girl, top of the class in most subjects, fiercely hard-working and very conscientious too. If she carried on progressing the way she had this year at school, her teachers said, there was a very good chance she'd pass the 11 plus and secure a place at the local grammar. After that, for someone with her splendid array of talents, so her teachers said, the world would be her oyster. Though she rarely revealed this to anyone other than God, she loved school and learning and had promised herself that she would always try her best to make the most of whatever educational opportunities came her way. Come what may, she was going to make something good of her life.

And there was her faith too, strong and sure and steady like her heartbeat. Though she was no musician herself and, she'd admit, no great singer, when she heard her church choir singing together on a Sunday she always felt deeply moved. And when mother, father and her younger brother had visited the great cathedral in town and heard its full choir singing, accompanied by the magnificent cathedral organ,

---

43

as those beautiful voices had risen in chorus up to the high, vaulted ceiling and jewelled sunlight had streamed through the big stained-glass windows and onto the cold, stone floor, she just knew she'd been granted a glimpse of the eternal.

✳

It had come as a bit of a shock when Anne's older brother, Terry, had come running and found them all in the park where they had been playing an epic game of hide-and-seek to tell her, breathlessly, that his mother wanted to see her immediately and that she was to go straightaway up to the house. She had looked at Anne for some clue as to what this could mean, but Anne just shrugged hers shoulders and didn't seem to know either, or wouldn't say.

So they had all trailed through the fields and up the lanes to the big white house at the top of the hill where Anne lived. While Susan and Anne chatted quietly and the boys goofed around she didn't join in. She couldn't help feeling anxious. They'd been friends since starting primary school together, but she'd only rarely been invited to play at Anne's and had never been invited inside their house. She hardly knew Anne's mother at all. She couldn't have said much more than hello and goodbye and thanks for having me to her in the whole time they'd been friends. Try as she might, she also just couldn't think of why Anne's mother would want to speak to her specifically. Was she perhaps in trouble or some sort? If she had done something wrong, she couldn't think of what it could be. Or, worse, she suddenly thought with alarm, had something bad happened at home? But, why then would Anne's mother be telling her? Oh, she really hoped nothing bad had happened at home.

It was with a head full of worries that she stood at the front door of

Anne's imposingly large house and watched as her friend reached up to ring the doorbell. As she waited, she twisted a daisy uneasily between her fingers.

After she'd left school and met a whole new world of people at university, she'd come to realise that this little gaggle of primary school friends weren't really from that much higher a social status than her: Tommy's dad worked in the family business; Peter's dad was the local policeman; Anne's father worked as the manager in the bank in town. Probably Susan's father was the poshest - he had a Southern accent, worked in the local pharmacy and had gone to university. Even then, though she only had a dim sense of what the word meant, she felt strongly that one day she might like to go to a university, though nobody else in her family had ever been to such a rarefied place.

When Anne's mother finally came to the door, she quickly ushered her daughter inside and told the other three children, who were hanging back by the garden gate, to go off somewhere else and make themselves useful. Only once they'd closed the gate and skipped off down the street did Anne's mother turns her eye on her and speak to her directly.

If she worked hard enough, so everyone said, even a girl like her, from a humble background, could really make it in today's world. Society was changing fast and there just weren't the same barriers in the way that there used to be for people from her sort of background. Opportunities were opening up everywhere, like flowers blossoming.

'Right. I want a word with you, young lady.' They were standing at the doorway and it was clear that, though it had now started to rain lightly, Anne's mother had no intention of inviting her inside. 'Damage has been done to Anne's brand-new bike, that she had for her birthday,

---

scratches and worse, a badly buckled wheel. I think you know exactly what I'm talking about, young lady. I've spoken to the others... your friends. Let's just say I'll be speaking to your parents about this, let me tell you, as will Anne's father, when he gets home from the bank. We'll expect the repairs to be paid for.' Anne's mother frowned at her. 'Well, have you anything to say for yourself?'

She felt herself blushing deeply under Anne's mother's cold, hard stare.

'No? Well, now get off with you and be thankful I haven't given you the bloody good hiding you deserve.' And with that she'd slammed the door shut.

Even then, aged nine, she knew exactly why she'd got the blame. She knew it deep in her bones, felt it like a cold chill. She felt that coldness deep within her bones as she had walked, in the rain, on the long and lonely walk home.

And now, more than seven decades later, sitting in her own large, detached, middle class home, remembering, she felt that coldness still.

The Coldness, 2

And so, here he was then, on the train clattering along the tracks from Bath all the way to some northern town to visit a mother he hadn't even known was alive until just a few, sweet days ago. Hadn't Father always told him that his mother had died a long time ago, when he had been just a tiny baby? Certainly he could recall no memories of any mother at all. Though, officially speaking, Mrs. Carew was father's housekeeper, she'd operated as a kind of surrogate mama to him, up until he'd been sent off to boarding school, as soon as he was out of short trousers. Apart from the school matrons, cold, hard Mrs. Carew was the closest thing he'd had to a mother and so he imagined his real mother might be something like her perhaps - strict, a bit stiff, generally rather tiresome for a chap to have to be around.

Of course, father hadn't filled him in on all the gory background details, not yet. He knew only a little about his mother's incarceration in the lunatic asylum and he had been kept entirely in the dark about the court case that had led to her eventual release, despite his father's strenuous efforts. Nor did he know that in all the years she'd spent in the asylum his father had not visited his wife, not once. Terrified by the thought of being infected by her madness, his father had not visited her, nor his older brother either, his only brother who would live all his life in the same asylum after coming back from war with shell shock.

Relatives he never knew he had and probably didn't wish to know were to greet him at the train station in this Northern town and then drive him to their house, where, as he understood it, there, awaiting him would be the mysterious woman who was his supposedly long dead.

They'd recognise him, he was assured, because he would be dressed in his school blazer, smart trousers and the school cap, fitted snugly above his neat, trimmed hair.

Really what was a chap to make of it all? How was one supposed to feel? In truth, when father had told him his mother was alive and apparently so wanted to see him so desperately, he'd felt nothing much more than a sort of numbness. And then a sickly unease. Now as he looked out of the train window and the landscape gradually changed from rolling countryside to the grimly industrial, he hoped his Northern relatives wouldn't turn out to be impossibly coarse and uncouth or horribly poor. But his greatest fear was that this lunatic woman might bring some unimaginable shame onto him and his respectable family.

※

To be reunited with the child she'd had to give up as a baby when they'd taken her in would have, until recently, been beyond her wildest dreams. But after Nessie and husband had won the court case and she'd escaped, finally, from that terrible, hollow, deathly place, very kindly they had set her up in a comfortable little flat, just on the right, proper side of town, near the river and the racecourse. And with the skills she'd acquired during her time in the WAF during the war, she'd even picked up a secretarial job in a nice little solicitor's office. The pay wasn't a fortune, it was true, but she had always lived frugally, keeping well within her means and she had even managed to put aside some savings, for a rainy day. Or a special one.

Of course, she had instructed them how they must all dress as smartly as they could manage and to mind their p's and q's. Her son was, she informed them proudly, at one of the finest schools in England and she didn't want them showing her up in front of him. Years ago she'd issued similar instructions when, somewhat under duress, she'd invited her most respectable sibling, her elder sister, Nessie, and her fat little husband to her wedding at St. Martins. Her career in the WAF having progressed better than anyone could have ever had imagined, she'd ended up socialising with the officer class. Having worked determinedly to ditch her Northern working-class accent, she had married well, well above her supposed station. Hubby had been a wing commander, no less, and his family had a big place in Surrey and were, so he told her, very well-to-do indeed.

At that wedding, all those years ago, she'd been terrified Nessie or Arthur would blurt out the family's shameful past. A past she'd worked so hard to bury. All that grinding, demeaning poverty. She didn't want her husband and his parents to know about her father's death on the train tracks or about mother bringing the four of them up singlehanded, working all day and then scrubbing pub floors at night to try to make ends meet. So now, once again, would everyone please be on their very best behaviour? It was important they make the right sort of impression on her dear, long-lost son.

✳

A little portly man in an old-fashioned pin-striped suit and his broadly smiling wife in a big hat had picked him up at the station. His newly discovered aunt had embraced him warmly and his uncle had taken his hand and shaken it vigorously in his rough palm. Now they were in his uncle's saloon car on the way to their house. While they tried to make awkward polite conversation with him, he felt relieved that their car was almost new, comfortable enough and a tolerable make too. At least they weren't horribly poor, these new relations, it seemed. Their car

---

49

might not be in the same league as father's Daimler, of course, but still he found solace in the fact it was not embarrassingly cheap nor embarrassingly old. It was something to cling on to when a chap felt rather at sea. As they drove through the outskirts of the town, he began to hope that, perhaps, these hearty Northern relatives wouldn't turn out to be as impoverished or unsophisticated as he had feared.

Naturally, father hadn't told him a great deal about them. Only really where they lived and something about his uncle's line of work. Apparently he owned a shoe shop, or something along those lines. Certainly they were in trade and not, like father, from the professional classes. But, he knew, he mustn't hold that against them; their lack of social distinction was not their fault, really. Not everybody, father had reminded him, had had the benefits of the first-class education he was currently enjoying. He had had the sense then that father didn't really approve of these lowly relatives, let alone like them. A chap couldn't blame him really - they were from his mother's side, which clearly was the inferior side of the family. And his mother, he remembered with a shudder, was or had once been some sort of a nutcase.

Once again, he was pleasantly surprised when finally they drew up at the house. A really quite impressively sized building, solid if not exactly elegant, with large gardens to front and rear and set on a respectable, broad, tree-lined street. There was money, it seemed, in the shoe trade.

At the front door they were greeted by a short, pretty girl with dark hair and darker eyes, his cousin, who must be a few years older than him, he expected. She ushered them enthusiastically into the hallway and babbled away at him in a Northern accent as his aunt fussed around, taking his coat and bag and so forth.

After his aunt had taken and hung his cap and coat in the neat little cloakroom, they informed him that his mad mother was waiting for him, eagerly, in the sitting room. Out of delicacy, they would give mother and son a little time together alone and then come in with a nice pot of tea and some refreshments. How did that sound? It sounded absolutely terrible, but what was one supposed to do in such circumstances? There wasn't a rule book to turn to for this sort of thing.

His aunt smiled at him again and, picking a bit of fluff from his blazer, told him how smart and handsome he looked in his school uniform. And then without more ado, the door to the sitting room was opened and, with great trepidation and feelings of dread, in he went.

Hardly had he stepped through into the room or had time to take a look at her before the woman had risen quickly from her chair and rushed over to embrace him in her open arms. Stiffly he suffered her to hug him and to put her soft, warm hands on his face. Wetly she'd kissed his cheeks and his forehead and he realised that she was crying.

'My son,' she said, 'my darling son! Oh, my son.'

As she ushered him to sit on the flowery sofa next to her, it was with some relief that he had discovered that, even though she was terribly agitated and clearly emotionally overwrought, this old-looking woman who was his mother was really rather well turned out in a smart navy skirt and matching blouse. Moreover, when she had spoken to him, if one ignored the gushing sentiment, it was in an accent far more cultured and refined than that of his other Northern relatives.

That weekend this highly excitable and, he thought, indisputably somewhat unstable woman would go on to spend all her savings on him, every last penny. Proudly, she would take him to the priciest restaurant in town. They would have tea too at the Grosvenor Hotel. Lavishing him with gifts, proudly she'd buy him some new, stylish clothes, whole outfits, top to toe, from the most expensive and exclusive shops. In one madly intense weekend she would try to make up for fourteen years of absence, desperately trying to compress into every moment all the love she had stored up for him over that great empty expanse of years. There was nothing she would not do for him. He would even sleep in her bed in her small flat, while she slept, fitfully, on the sofa.

✻

At the train station they were saying their emotional goodbyes. Or rather she was. He'd allowed her to hug him again and, barely hiding his distaste, had had to accept yet another soggy kiss on his cheek. The poor woman was crying, again, and really he didn't want her to make yet another scene in public. He might feel sorry for her, but hadn't he already had to put up with a weekend of this? So then, it was with gratitude that he heard the train's whistle. Moments later and he was aboard it and setting off, gratefully, for home. Safely on his way back on the train to father and Mrs. Carew and then on to his reassuringly expensive, world-renowned boarding school.

As she watched her fine, handsome, oh-so dapper son clambering onto the train and then the train pulling steadily away from the station, with his dear hand, waving through the window, though she no longer had any faith, as she looked up and the late evening sun flashed in the high windows of the station and flashed again in the windows of the train, she prayed for the first time in years, prayed fervently that she should see him again and see him again soon.

But even then, in the chilly evening air, somewhere deep down in her heart, she knew this was the last time in her life that she would ever see her son.

Small Town Dreams

So here we are then, the four of us, the gang, standing on a street corner of our well-heeled, provincial, mega-dull-as-death hometown, sometime between eleven and midnight, in our best, gaudiest glad rags – flowery, frilly shirts, drain-pipe jeans, pixie boots, looking for all the world like callow rejects from the Blitz Club or, with the earrings, bouffant dyed hair and clumsily applied eyeliner, like a particularly inept *Duran Duran* tribute act.

The disco at the local youth club has recently finished. One of us, the cocky best-looking, bleached blond one, has danced and got off with a girl, much to his friends' bitter envy, and we're all a little bit tipsy on the pints of watered-down lager we've been allowed to drink, despite being underage. Now we're waiting for someone's father to come and pick us up and drive us safely home.

Even at the time it seems foolishly ill-advised for one of us, the short ex-Mancunian with the usually disarming, cheeky little boy's smile, to approach, before we can think to stop him, the large group of older, bigger boys now spilling noisily out from the doors of the Youth Club. What motivates this recklessness will always remain one of life's subtler mysteries, but we take comfort in the fact that our friend certainly means no harm. He's got balls, we have to admit, the complete and utter idiot. But what's the worst that could happen?

Nervously we watch our foolish friend as he walks perhaps a little unsteadily towards the large and rowdy group barrelling now down the road towards us, who, we see suddenly in the sickly yellow glow of the streetlights, all have the close-shaven crew-cuts, the bomber jackets,

---

turned-up jeans and big bovver boots that are the unmistakable uniform of skinheads.

Crickey-O'Reilly, we think in unison. This might not turn out too well.

We could run. We should have run. But, inexplicably, we don't run. Instead we remain where we are, rooted to the spot as we are confronted suddenly by the large group of baying skinheads, moving up uncomfortably close.

Long-haired, girly, pop star wannabes, we are too young, too naïve; we have led such sheltered lives. We have never been attacked before or faced any real violence. We do not really know what to expect and stand around not knowing quite what to do with ourselves. Like particularly stupid sheep surrounded by a pack of ravenous wolves.

Until one of the pack of skinheads, a small, stocky, particularly angry one, strides up to the tallest of us, plants his legs wide in a boxing stance, cocks his arms by his sides, sticks out his chin and puffs out his chest.

'Are you the leader?' the little skinhead spits out gruffly.

Confronted like this, you don't know what to say. The leader? Despite your size, you're a gentle, sensitive soul. You're not looking for any trouble. You don't know what the right response might be. You really don't mean to betray your best friend, but still the words come spilling out of your mouth before you can stop them.

'No. He is,' you say, nodding slightly towards your blond-haired friend.

Who sees all too clearly now that this ugly, angry little skinhead is going

---

55

to stride up and try to headbutt him in the face. And, as this does indeed happen, it seems as though the bullet-head swings back almost in slow motion. The intended headbutt starts from the pivot of the hips, the whole torso tipping mechanically backwards and then takes a long swing forwards. Fortunately, he is good at sport and his reflexes must be pretty sharp, because he easily sidesteps the rather maladroit headbutt, swaying aside like he might to miss a fast bouncer in a school cricket match.

None of the four of us can recall exactly what happens next. There is, however, what might be called something of a violent melee.

The blond one might or might not have punched the skinhead and might or might not have knocked his assailant to the ground. Definitely he sees someone swinging a motorcycle helmet in a wide, sickening arc, aimed at one of his friends' heads. Fortunately it misses its target and, instead, bounces thuddingly off the tarmac. Simultaneously he sees too that some of the skinheads have somehow picked up bricks and are holding them in their hands.

He shouts one word, as loud as he can: 'RUN!'

Then, as one, we are all hurtling down the street, away from the town lights, running for our lives, hell-for-leather, not knowing where we are heading, just legging it away as fast as our legs can carry us. Behind, we can hear a hail of objects being hurled, bricks, helmets, bottles and god-knows-what else, that come smashing and crashing to the ground around their running feet.

Blindly we run and run into the dark, the adrenalin pumping like electricity in our veins. Until, eventually, we realise we're not being pursued and can pause to catch our racing breaths, panting like dogs, suddenly alone in a dark, silent side street, standing staring at each other. What to do next? No sounds of pursuit. Not yet, anyway. But we know, we're not safe yet. If there were motorcycle helmets, there must be scooters too.

✳

It is a miracle, the workings of an extraordinary grace and providence, when, out of the blue, a car pulls up to us and, with a flood of relief, we recognise the driver as one of our friends' dads. Our friend's dad winds down the window and tells us to jump in quickly and motions us over. He tells us that he'd heard from his son that there has been trouble at the Youth Club - vandalism, fights breaking out, general thuggishness - and, as responsible citizen, he has come to see if he can do anything to help.

'Don't worry, lads, you're all safe now. I'll drive you home,' he says.

A guardian angel, sent from heaven.

We are so grateful, so relieved, so still in shock, that we can hardly speak.

✳

Sitting in the back of the car as they drive steadily back through the streets, his head is still buzzing with the fear and the exhilaration and the sweet, sweet relief, and is, therefore, taken by surprise when the car is flagged down by a powerfully built young man in a pork pie hat standing at the side of the road. He really doesn't want Mr. Hussein to stop, but what can he do? What can he say about the terrible dread he's already feeling in the pit of his stomach?

Ever the good, solid citizen, of course Mr. Hussein pulls over, winds down the car's passenger window, leans over and asks the young man what the hell's going on. Menacingly the pork pie hat guy pushes his ugly mug in through the car window, ignores Mr. Hussein entirely and scans the friends huddled together, cowering in the half-light in the back seats. Then he sniffs the air like an animal.

'I'm looking for the cunt who beat up my mate. When I find him, I'm going kick his fucking head in.'

Though he remains admirably calm, we can tell Mr. Hussein is shocked and maybe even scared. Savagery comes off the young man like a toxic reek. But, calmly, Mr. Hussein informs him that he is a police officer [which we know he isn't] and tells him to get himself home before he calls his colleagues out to deal with him. If there's any more trouble tonight, he's seen his face and now he knows what he looks like. Pork pie hat guy snarls at him, like a dangerous dog. But Mr. Hussein winds up the window and drives off, more quickly this time.

In the backseat, I am 100% sure that pork pie hat guy was out looking for me.

Remembering the Future

And here he is again, as they've come recently to dread, knocking gently but insistently on the door of their single room, as he has almost every night for the last month or more, their new, frankly rather creepy co-resident, in the terraced house they share with a group of disparate strangers on a rundown street in Catford, South London, in the year of our lord 1993.

He'd pop his head around the door. He'd want to come in and watch whatever they were watching on TV and smoke a few fags, maybe have a cup of tea and a natter. If it wasn't a programme he understood or held his interest, he'd really want to talk, delivering long, winding monologues without much need of interruption. He didn't have his own TV and the house was without a communal room and without much communal spirit either. None of the others would let him in; they weren't so soft as these two alternative, studenty types. This was before the internet or mobile phones and their co-resident didn't have much capacity to entertain himself, other than by dancing manically in the kitchen to dance tunes blasting out the radio.

Hearing the knocking, they whisper to each other, consulting like conspirators. They don't want to be unfriendly, but even so. They knew he was needy, but this is already getting too much. It happens every night now. Ruefully, they knew they were an easy target and now their kindness is being exploited. She tells him he should really say something, that sometimes they should say no, make a stand. They are being used, they know it. It wouldn't be rude to say no, would it? They're a couple and needed some privacy. That is only fair. He'd understand that, surely. It isn't too much to ask, is it? And then they let him in, again.

This house, these residents, that place. It really got them down. How had their bright, promising lives washed up here, like a shipwreck of all hopes? They had so little money, this room in this house in this place was all they could afford. She is doing a Masters; he's training to be a teacher. They are still living and eating like students, but not with friends as at university, having fun, but here, miserably, in Catford, with complete strangers.

There was the sweet, quiet, reclusive black girl who lived in the largest room at the top of the house. She'd smile anxiously at them whenever their paths crossed and exchange a few polite, guarded words. One time they'd had to call an ambulance when she knocked on their door and told them that she'd taken some pills. She'd told them, as the most responsible people in the house, because she thought they'd help. After that, she left, for good.

And also the spectacularly sour, foul-mouthed girl, training to do something or other at college, to do with accounts, or she claims, while working as a receptionist at some kind of dodgy hotel. They never believe a word she said. The world is so stacked against her, everything is unfair, her merits have never recognized. She has a genius IQ, she tells them, she dropped out of Uni, though promised a first. Podgy feet crammed into too tight shoes, pasty-faced, she has a violent aversion to the fruit and vegetables they store in the fridge and a love for Pot Noodles and the ready-to-eat mashed potato she has come to resemble. If anyone has the temerity to be in the shower in the one communal bathroom and this girl needs it, they'll hear her pacing up and down the hallway, cursing loudly, making threats, sometimes banging on the door to hurry the fuck up will you, you selfish motherfuckers.

There'd been others. Some guy who worked away most of the time. An older guy who they'd hardly seen. But this new, creepy one, the one now knocking insistently on their bedroom door, again, he really is something else, he really is at a whole different level.

Troy is his name, or so he claims. A couple of years older than them, maybe in his late twenties, he'd been released from prison after serving time for attempted GBH, or perhaps just GBH. As far as they could ascertain, he was on some sort of controlled release scheme, at least that's what the landlord had hurriedly assured them. Coming out of prison, Troy had almost no possessions - a couple of pairs of tracksuit bottoms, a few t-shirts and a manky old coat, two mugs and a jar for tea, that was about the lot. That was all he had to face the world. Just enough to fill the adidas hold-all they'd lent him shortly before he'd disappeared.

Whenever they got home from school or college, Troy would be in the kitchen waiting for them in his grubby vest and low-slung adidas trackies, chain-smoking cheap fags. Ashen-faced, scrawny, perpetually itchy, he never looked healthy. He told them he had a real problem with boils. Like some medieval sinner, he was plagued by boils, particularly, he told them, at the point where the base of his spine met the top of his backside. Helpfully he would show them, unless they told him, firmly, not to.

As they put down their bags, embraced and put the kettle on, breathlessly he'd tell them all about his day, from getting up and getting out of bed and then making himself a cup of tea to the moment they'd just arrived there that minute. First when his alarm had gone off, he'd gotten up, see, and out of bed, pulled on his trackies and then headed into the kitchen. There he'd got out a tea bag from the cupboard, making sure it was from his own store and not from anyone else's and then put the teabag in his own cup, filled the kettle up with water, to about halfway, so as not to waste electricity, see, turned it on at the socket and then waited impatiently for something else to do.

Once the kettle had finally boiled, see, he'd taken it and poured the hot water into cup onto the teabag and then waited again, this time only for a short time, and then spooned out the bag, gone to the fridge, found the small carton of milk with his name scribbled on it and added just a drop. Then he'd put the milk back in the fridge, if there was any left. Troy liked his tea sweet, really sweet, so next he'd add three heaped spoonfuls of sugar. Smashing. Fucking super.

Eventually, after perhaps a month of visitations every evening, they'd saved a week's worth of rent to buy him his own TV. Taken him down to the second-hand electrical goods store in the arcade next to the shop selling knives and bought him a big TV of his own for £25. Though they couldn't afford it, but it was worth every penny.

Sometimes Troy'd have some of his new-found mates round, sometimes in the middle of the night and early hours of the morning. One of the couple might wander into the kitchen to make a cuppa or to ask what the noise was and could they turn it down please because some people had to get up and go to work in the morning and find them dancing, completely off their trolleys, buzzing, lit-up, eyes unfocused and bloodshot, just babbling, on something neither of them liked to imagine.

And then one night he tells them about the terrible, potentially fatal, car crash his older brother has had. Hit hard by a lorry on an A-road at night. The car is a complete right-off. His brother's in hospital fitting for his life, but, tragically, isn't expected to survive. So Troy needs desperately to get back home as quick as possible to see his dying

---

brother and support his mother in her grief. They offer comfort, lend him the hold-all and the money for the train fare back home and then he disappears off into the night on his errand of mercy.

The next morning when they go into his room they find it stripped bare. He'd never had much. But all of it has gone. No clothes, no possessions, no furniture, no clothes, no cups, no big tele.

Later the landlord tells them how he'd tried to trace Troy, who owed money for his rent, of course. Tells them how he'd rung the mother a couple of hours ago to ask about the brother's accident and express his sincere condolences. Troy it seems has told him that his brother has died. He feels bad about it, but he was relieved that Troy has even given him the right number. But, no, Troy's mother hasn't seen him in at all, not in six months or more. And, no, there's been no accident. In fact, Troy has no brother. Troy has never had a brother.

He might not have been smart, but it turned out Troy was a first-class bullshitter, spinning a sad, sad story or, perhaps, relaying one he'd been told to tell with jittery and tearful conviction. Crying and chain-smoking the whole evening.

They chalk it down to experience. Worry what might have happened to Tory. Why did he need to disappear so suddenly like that? And then they got back on track to realising their promising futures.

But, for a good while they find themselves still listening each evening for that gentle but insistent knocking on their bedroom door.

That Blake Bloke

#1

It was just so much more awkward whenever he was around. Before he arrived on the scene the four of us, we could talk comfortably, just chat unselfconsciously about whatever was on our minds. Didn't amount to much perhaps, this and that. We were just chewing the fat, whatever was on our minds. With him hunched over a book in the corner or tapping away at that damned computer, we felt judged, that our conversation was not really worthy of his supposedly more refined attention. As if everything we said was just empty-headed piffle.

And, yes, I did resent that. I don't mind telling you, I really resented it. Don't we all need a break sometimes? God, didn't we deserve it? A chance to let our hair down and relax over a spot of lunch and maybe a bit of juicy gossip. Of course, we did. And he just ruined it.

#2

To be fair, I think he may have found our conversation a bit dull. Middle-aged women and him being quite a bit younger and, obviously, male. Not that I wasn't capable of discussion on a more erudite level, of course, but I choose not to, not during my down time. I need the light relief, you see. He could be quite witty too, I admit, in a clever clogs sort of way, but I never felt entirely relaxed talking to him. He might be poking fun and you might not entirely realise. Snidey, bit of a clever clogs, pleased with himself, if you know what I mean. Liked to present himself as a freethinker - I think he was probably an atheist too, which is his lookout, of course. But, you know the type.

#3

No, he was good with my son, I have to say that, in his defence. Best teacher Gary ever had, that's what Gary said. And I found him quite quiet and considerate too, mostly. But, if riled, he could be sharp-tongued. Obviously. And this time, things he just went far too far.

#4

Well, we started at the same time and I'm younger than the other three. I have to admit I also tired sometimes of their chit chat - the endless gossip, the limited and repetitive round of topics. But what got me was their endless moaning. Jeez, they could moan for England those three. I know it wound him up, especially as they'd always be complaining about how this or that was wrong, but never speak up to the managers or do anything about it. You know, honestly, sometimes I think they enjoyed nothing more than having something to have a really good whinge about. Well, he gave them that, in spades, didn't he?

#1

Okay, to be truthful here, I was a bit anxious around him, mainly in case he'd discover about the computer. Ask me something about the schemes of work he'd been re-writing busily, modernising to get them up to his supposedly superior standards. I never used the damned thing and never wanted to. Still haven't. To tell you the truth, I was a bit afraid I'd damage it somehow. Sounds stupid, I suppose, but I'd just never got round to learning how to use it. And there he was bashing away all through lunch, typing whatever. So, I hadn't ever read any of his work. Which put me on edge with him, a bit, I suppose.

#6

Mmm, I see. Very helpful.
But, please, tell me more…

#2

He'd let pupils come to the door to talk to him. At lunchtimes. That was a big no-no for us. None of us liked to see that. We worked like trojans during lesson times, flogged ourselves near to death. Not that we got much thanks from anyone for that, of course. And didn't expect it. But our lunchtimes were sacrosanct. We needed to recover our energy, sometimes recover from battling a difficult class. We didn't want some needy tyke turning up asking for some extra help with his homework, disturbing our breaktime.

#3

Don't think they'd admit it, but the other two felt that he was showing them up. They'd been here forever and they never allowed pupils to come to the staffroom door during lunch or break. He was far too keen and obliging with his time, to the pupils that is. It made the rest of us look bad. Certainly made me feel inadequate. Sometimes you know I think he found them more interesting to talk to than us, the pupils.

#4

That day? Jeez, it's hard to remember. I think it was something about the price of sprouts. ----------- is a big sprout fan, loves them, though, apparently, they give her wind, or so she was saying. She was saying something about the price going up, or perhaps down, on the market. Can't remember. I wasn't really listening very closely, to be honest.

#1

Don't get me wrong, I like to talk about literature and books, just not all the blasted time. And certainly not like that. Not it that way. It's not, respectable. It's just not, well, very nice is it.

#2

I'm more of a classic novel fan myself. For pleasure? Can't beat a good historical novel, with a cup of cocoa, curled up in bed. Suits me down to the ground. Nothing too raunchy, mind you.

I don't approve of smut.

#1
And that, that was definitely smutty. Very smutty.

#3
Oh yes, I love Blake, though I'm not sure I fully understand most of his poems. Who does? He was a bit of a nutter, wasn't he, by all accounts? So, yes, I was listening in. Malheureusement.

#6
A bit of a smutty nuttter? I see, yes. Go on...

#1
Well, as if we wanted to hear about his brilliant lessons with the Sixth Formers when we were trying to eat our sandwiches in peace.

#6
From these notes, I see, they are telling us he used to paint the pictures of the people, always the people with the huge black hands. When he was only a small, only a little child. The huge black hands.

#2
He was just showing-off, that's all, showing-off and showing us up.

#6
Then later, the long, dyed hair and the earrings. Interesting, very interesting... The rose that was sick, you say?

———

#1

Yes, that's right. That's the poem he was supposedly 'discussing'. As if anyone we wanted to talk about poetry, in our break time.

#2

And a very sick rose, if you ask me, the way he read it. Disgusting. Absolutely disgusting.

#6

The rose that is being sick? Most interesting…

#3

Well, it's about a flower that, though it looks healthy on the outside, has, shall we say, been corrupted from the inside.

#6

Healthy on the outside and corrupted from within? Interesting, most, most interesting…

#1

And it was his 'interpretation' of the poem that he suddenly shared with us, completely out of the blue, without any by-your-leave. Well, I tell you, I've never read that poem in that way. Frankly, it's obscene. Shocking. Completely ruined the poem for me.

#2

He just came right out with it, without any prior warning, while we were still in the middle of eating our lunch. Disgusting. What he was saying, I mean, not the lunch. Absolutely disgusting.

#4

Honestly, I nearly choked on my ham sarnie.

#3

I know that I turned bright red. I was that embarrassed. Didn't know where to look. Thought I might not have heard right. I mean, excusez moi?

#4

I'm afraid I laughed out loud. But when I saw the other's faces, like stone they were, I stopped straightaway, of course. Jeez, they really were not happy. Not happy at all.

#1

Tried to claim his so-called 'interpretation', that filth, was influenced by some American feminist literary critic, Paglia-something or other.

#2

Camile Pagli…? Or was it Camilia Paglia? Something like that.

#1

Whatever.

As if that justifies it.

#4

Yes, well, it's Camille Paglia… She might be Italian, I think?

#6

Camille Paglia? Interesting. Very interesting… And this interpretation suggests that, what?

#1

That Blake's poem…

—

#2

...'The Sick Rose'...

#3

...is really about...

#2

Do we really have to say it?

#6

Yes. Tell me please... Go on...

#4

...well, is really about the secret pleasures of... of.... self, erm. I'm trying to put this as delicately as possible, unlike he did, of course, the secret pleasure of, erm, self-pleasuring...

#6

Oh! I think I see... You mean?

#1, 2, 3 & 4

Yes!

#6

Interesting... of the female, what shall we say, variety?

#1, 2, 3 & 4

Yes!

#1

And during our lunch hour...

#2

While we were innocently trying to eat our sandwiches…

#1 & #2

Disgusting.

#3

So completely inappropriate…

#4

Really, just, you know, hilarious. But I didn't know where to look…

#6

Interesting. Most interesting… So, let us sum up: if I have got this right, this Blake poet is erm… What you are telling me is that this Blake poet, must have been what you English are calling a right dirty old bugger, yes? Interesting. How very interesting…

A Reasonable Adjustment

- You wanted to see me Headmaster?
- Oh yes, Mr. Croft come in, come in. Do take a seat. There's no need to look so worried - you're not in any trouble, honestly.
- Oh good, thanks. That's a relief!
- I'm sure. So you must be wondering what this is all about. Let me not beat about the bush and come straight to the point, without any further delay or pointless prevarication. Not to put too fine a point on it, I've had reports from the school's SNUD department that you aren't really following their policies very closely.
- Oh really, I'm sorry, in what ways specifically?
- Well, I'm told, and you may of course deny it if you wish or provide evidence to the contrary, that you've not been making reasonable adjustments for pupils who might face particular challenges in your subject.
- Really? That doesn't sound great. I'm so sorry. Could you give me some specific examples?
- Of course: Giving extra time to complete tasks, breaking instructions down to more manageable chunks, providing a support teacher, that sort of thing. Standard practice in other words.
- Right, but in what context exactly haven't I been doing this?
- The 100 metres race you organised last week has been somewhat mentioned.
- The 100 metres?
- Yes, according to my sources, you didn't make any allowances at all for pupils who are not-yet-so-fast at running and therefore need a bit more help and support than the other, shall we say, pace-advantaged children.

- Sorry, I'm not sure that I follow.

- Well, that rather does prove the point then, doesn't it, I'm afraid. It says quite clearly in our school SNUD policy, a policy which, by the way, has won many plaudits from parents and pupils alike, that pupils who are slower processors than others should be given more time to complete any set task. This appears not to have been the case with the race you organised during your recent P.E lesson.

- Sorry, Headmaster, but I'm not quite clear about how I should have made reasonable adjustments in the case of a running race.

- Well, I would have thought that was entirely self-evident, if you'd read our policy properly Mr. Croft. Either the slower pupils could start the race earlier or have more time to complete it than their, can we agree, faster, peers. I presume you are familiar, Mr. Croft with the concept of extra time?

- Extra time?

- Yes, extra time, in order to complete tasks. Naturally, some of your pupils need extra time to complete their 100 metres, I'm sure you will agree. Unfortunate though it may be, that is inevitably the case.

- Well, I suppose...

- Please also inform me what provision you have put in place for any pupils who find co-ordinating their legs, feet and arms in motion difficult to achieve, especially at moderate to high speeds and within rigidly straight lines? Have you tried breaking down this task into its component parts, starting perhaps with some simple low-stakes hand movement exercises? Or did you jump straight in at the deep end and somehow expect the pupils to magically not drown?

- Drown? They weren't swimming, Headmaster.

- There's no need to be facetious, Mr. Croft, I know very well that they weren't swimming. I was speaking metaphorically. You haven't answered my question.

- But these pupils opted to take GCSE P.E. Headmaster...

- That's as maybe, but it doesn't mean that some of them don't need

---

73

a bit more support than others, now does it?

- …and we're a specialist sports college.

- Well, that rather supports my point. Does it not? In his infinite wisdom, The Good Lord has not distributed talents evenly, I think you'll agree, Mr. Croft. Our SNUD department also wants me to emphasise to you that SNUD is not just something that only affects pupils at the not-yet-at-the-top end of the ability range, a very common misconception, I'm afraid, it also affects the needs of those more fortunately able and their needs also need to be catered for. I would like, therefore, to know what additional stretch and challenge you have been providing for the high starter pupils in your class.

- Well, I… I'm not sure how I…

- Come, come Mr. Croft. It's simple enough. It just needs a bit of creative thinking. Could you not simply make the 100 metres longer, by, perhaps, 20% for your high starter runners, or, perhaps, tie one of their legs to the other one, or make them run backwards perhaps. I have it - better still and far more simple - simply give them less time to complete the race. And see how one creative solution neatly suggests another? Why not make your, shall we say, more challenged pupils run 75 rather than the conventional 100 metres? What is convention in any case, other than yesterday's outmoded rules? That does seem to me like a perfectly reasonable adjustment. 25% dispensation is, of course, as you must know, standard practice in many examinations.

- Really, Headmaster, I have to say…

- So sorry to cut you off, Mr. Croft, but the 100 metres dash is not the only example provided by the SNUD department of your failure to adequately follow school SNUD policies. Apparently, you have not been lowering the bar for the high jump nor providing any rest breaks during the 400, 800 nor even the 1600 metres.

- Rest breaks?

- Of course. Standard SNUD practice. Don't you realise that some of our pupils find moving for long periods of time in a co-ordinated fashion and in one, uniform direction very difficult due to problems with cognitive load, memory incapacity, attention deficit, interest deficiency and similar challenges. Rest periods are therefore essential. Otherwise, some pupils would be unfairly penalised for their physical not-yet-fitness. You must see that surely.

- Look, Headmaster, I'm all for, dispensations, for pupils with genuine needs, but how do we know which ones are genuine?

- Simple. The parents pay for an independent external assessor who confirms that this is the case.

- Right. Okay Headmaster. I see. Is that all?

- I'm afraid it is not. As you should know by now, Mr. Croft, some pupils find the pressure of performing in group situations very challenging. Where possible, SNUD dictates that reasonable measures should be taken to accommodate such needs.

- Well, yes, Headmaster, but I don't see how this...

- The football and netball teams, Mr. Croft. Is it not painfully obvious? What reasonable provision have you made for some of these pupils to carry out their tasks free from the constant pressure of the expectations of their peers? As you know, teenagers can be very tough on each other and it is our job, I hope you will agree, to offer some protection. Mr. Croft, I am talking about separate spaces. Rather than being lumped together on the same field, pitch or whatever, en masse, some pupils need a separate space to play their sport. We are talking individual action plans, personalised learning Mr. Croft. That makes perfect sense, I'm sure you agree.

- Well I...

- Now we are really on a roll, Mr. Croft. You are aware that in other lessons, some SNUD pupils have even greater support, such as use of a laptop. Let's go back to those races you insist on running. As we've been talking, I've had most wonderful idea. Why could you not find a speedy support teacher who could carry the differently paced pupils during the race? The pupil could ride the teacher, like a jockey on a

———

horse. That would not only be fun, it would foster excellent pupil to staff relations. An educational double win, if I do say so myself. Mind you, if more mechanical support is required, why not allow these pupils to ride a bike, or better still, a golf cart or some such suitably speedy and comfortable vehicle? That really would make a much more level playing field, would it not? Though, perhaps there would be budget implications to consider. But what is money, other than a means to an end, Mr. Croft? Reasonable adjustment, Mr. Croft, that should be the name of your game, reasonable adjustment.

- Yes, Headmaster. Of course, Headmaster.

Learning with Style

The eagerly awaited data had finally come through on her new class. According to this data, several pupils had no confirmed or definite preference of learning style. As usual, the dominants were the visual and auditory learners, which was fine, she thought, as most of her lessons naturally catered for these preferences. The physical learners were a bit more of a challenge in English. She could get them up and about the classroom, though that introduced a disciplinary dimension to an already challenging situation, but she felt she should be able to cope by now. But the last two preferences on the list were the first she'd had in her short teaching career. Olfactory learners? What the hell was she supposed to do with olfactory learners?

Worse still, when she cross-referenced with their GMS score, she knew that making progress with these two was going to be a challenge. Already both pupils had exhibited clear signs of having stubbornly FMSs, a disposition which ran entirely contrary to the whole growth ethos expounded with tremendous enthusiasm by almost everyone in her new school. One of the DHTs was i/c GMS, so he really wouldn't be happy to have pupils in yr.10, after months of school assemblies devoted almost entirely to the topic, still displaying such stubbornly negative FMSs.

To be honest, she probably wouldn't even have known what 'olfactory' meant if learning styles hadn't been part of her teaching training and induction as an NQT. Meanwhile she knew GMS was the bright new thing, but, in private, over a glass of wine, would admit to friends that she had doubts as to whether, once you stripped away the

---

77

terminology, it really amounted to very much. Not that she'd say such heresy out loud in her new school. The more zealous GMS adherents of the common room would probably stone her alive.

A happy thought occurred to her. Perhaps the English department's s.o.w. on the Scottish play already had lessons tailored to different types of learning styles and have been designed to overcome the rigid negative thinking of a FMS. Eagerly she scanned through the available documentation. Unfortunately, the s.o.w., it seemed, had not been updated to accommodate the revelation of learning styles. It talked in unenlightened and outmoded terms, of 'bringing out the drama' in scenes, ways in which 'characters are compelling' and about the exploring 'patterns of imagery as prompts for thematic concerns' and such like old hat. Anxiously, she searched for any references at all to olfactory learning or overcoming an unhealthily FMS through the power of Shakespeare's words and found nothing. Perhaps she could ask one of her English teaching colleagues for help? Yes, but she didn't want to appear uninformed or incompetent.

And, perhaps, she should see this gap in the s.o.w. as an opportunity, a chance to impress. She was only a few weeks into her probationary year and it wasn't definite that her new school would keep her if she didn't do well enough with her classes. Her new HoD seemed nice but he was also very demanding and always too busy to give her much time. Revising the 'Macbeth' s.o.w. to incorporate learning styles and to promote a healthy GMS would show initiative and might earn some useful brownie points.

Now another thought struck her: she'd not found any mention in the 'Macbeth' s.o.w. either of nurturing emotional resilience, which she'd understood had to be built into all her English teaching, nor any mention at all about maintaining British values and combating the dangers of terrorism. Do these things have to be taught explicitly, she wondered. If so, despite her recent training, she wasn't really quite sure how. Could Macbeth himself be seen as a defender of British values, defending the island against European invaders, perhaps? But, then, back in those days was Scotland even part of Great Britain? She'd have to check that. Another thought: Could regicide and, specifically, the killing of King Duncan be read as an act of domestic terrorism? That seemed entirely plausible. But then, wouldn't that make Macbeth both a defender of British values and also a terrorist? Crumbs, that might be rather confusing for her class. Perhaps she ought to put these issues to one side for the moment.

Olfactory learning, that was the major stumbling block. That's what she needed to focus on. Another thought popped into her head: Hold on one minute, how would olfactory learners be catered for in another subject? She'd already made a friend in Maths, a guy who had started the school at the same time as her and had a nice, self-deprecating sense of humour and a sweet, shy smile. Perhaps she could ask him. It might be a failure of training or imagination, she reflected ruefully, but she just couldn't think how to teach something like quadratic equations through the power of smell.

Certainly she didn't envy him that. In that respect, she realised now, with a sigh of relief, English was far easier. Now that she really thought about it, weren't there a lot of smells in 'Macbeth'? Yes, there were! Loads of smells! With a growing sense of excitement, she realised that 'Macbeth' was, in fact, a very smelly play.

＊

Fortunately the 'Macbeth' lesson was scheduled for after break, so she had had a good twenty minutes to prepare the classroom. Getting hold of enough blood had been a stiff challenge, of course, but one she took professional pride in having risen to. Once she'd had the idea for the lesson, she'd spent weeks collecting it, from various sources. She had only needed a bowlful. Mostly she'd collected animal blood, the last of which she'd drained from some cheap steaks. When this hadn't look quite enough, she'd been forced to supplement it with some blood of her own. Swilling the red liquid around gently in the bowl on her desk, she noticed now for the first time how strongly it smelled. Kind of metallic and sort of rusty.

She'd kept the 'Macbeth' olfactory lesson a big secret and then, with barely suppressed excitement, had invited her new HoD to come and observe her teach it. She hoped it would make a big splash with the pupils, especially the two FMS kids, and also, fingers firmly crossed, leave a spectacular impression on her boss.

As well as the blood, in various vessels, arranged on tables around the room were other pungent delights for the class to experience and learn from. She was especially pleased with her symbol for the theme of corruption – a bowl of wriggling maggots which she'd bought online from a well-known retailer. As well as having a truly horrid stink, these would also appeal to the class's more tactile learners, a secondary learning style preference, the data said, of a number of the pupils.

✳

The Headteacher regarded her from underneath his half-rimmed spectacles and, she noticed, rather bushy, unkempt eyebrows. Her end-of-year assessment had come so much earlier than she had been led to expect. Apparently, having an end-of-year assessment in your first term as an NQT was almost unheard of, or so everyone said. Nervously fiddling with her fingers in her lap, now she was waiting for the Headteacher to speak. She could see he had some of kind of report open on the desk before him, but, though she tried to sneak a glance, it was too difficult to read what the upside-down words upside. There did, however, appear to be some red ink and some capital letters.

The Headteacher stroked his beard ruminatively. 'The lesson supposedly about 'Macbeth', Miss Newinny,' he began eventually, 'I really need to talk to you about that.' He sounded, she thought, rather tired, the poor man.

'In particular,' he began again, looking at directly her for the first time and running a hand through his thinning hair, 'to be frank, in all my years in teaching, really I've never heard of anything like it.'

That could be good, she thought. Original. Originality is good. Usually. Isn't it? That was something to cling to. Certainly her HoD had been left stunned, he said, by her lesson. Afterwards he'd been almost literally speechless. But, it was hard to tell exactly, as he hadn't been in school since then.

Now the Headmaster cleared his throat and leant forward in his chair towards her, 'Miss Newinny, I need to talk to you about the blood, about something you called the 'witches' brew' and also, dear God in Heaven, about all that copious vomiting...'

The Snap

The first move was a note left one day on his desk. Though it was unpleasant to receive such a message, it hadn't worried him, not unduly. Not at the time. Only in retrospect did it seem so much more ominous and threatening. It read, simply, 'we don't like you'. He'd looked at the small, torn scrap of paper and read the simple scribbled words with a slight sense of shock. Then he'd studied the handwriting, but had not been able to determine the writer, or writers, from the crude block capitals. Where was the paper from? Hard to tell. Photocopier perhaps. Having screwed it up, he was about to chuck the note in the bin when he stopped and had second thoughts. Perhaps he should keep it, just in case, as potential evidence. Though evidence for what, he couldn't really imagine.

The rest of that day it hadn't worried him overmuch, though he had read the note again before he left for home in the evening. After telling his wife about it over dinner, he had gone to sleep soundly enough, relatively untroubled. Julie told him not to take it too seriously, certainly not to take it to heart. Perhaps it was somebody's bad idea of a joke. Even if it wasn't, you couldn't be popular with everyone all the time, and some people, she said, even children, could be cruel. Surely he knew that well enough. He was a bit of a sensitive soul, inclined to take things too seriously. So she'd encouraged him to try to laugh about it over a nice glass of cold wine. Then a new thought had occurred. A comforting thought. How did they even know the note was addressed to him? There was no mention of any name. Perhaps one of the cleaners had found it and put it on his desk, not knowing what else to do with it. Yes, that could be it. It was a note sent from one pupil to

—

82

another, perhaps. That made sense, certainly.

After the drive into school, with a journey spent listening to all the terrible things going in the world on the radio, by the time he was sitting back at his desk the following morning, he'd forgotten about it, almost. And, indeed, life had gone on normally, for a day or two. As the business of the day unfolded, slowly the message faded from his attention and he had stopped turning it over and over in his mind.

Until a second one arrived, a few days later. The same crude block capitals, in the same black ink - probably a biro he now realised. Another scrap of torn white paper, placed on his desk, right in front of his computer, this time, so he couldn't possibly miss it. This time there was no room for doubt - the note was certainly addressed to him. Just three words: 'We're watching you'.

A more unnerving message, for sure. But, this time, he was more angry than concerned, initially at least. Why would anyone send him a message like that? Who'd send it? What did it even mean exactly? So what if someone was watching him? He had nothing to hide, not really, no more than anybody else. Why should he care? It was ridiculous. He wasn't going to let himself be worried by something so absurd. If it was meant to scare him, well, it wasn't working was it and it wasn't going to work. Yes, intense irritation was the main emotion he felt. Who were these anonymous we? He tried to think of anyone who might have a grudge against him or anyone he'd had a recent run-in with. But came up with nothing. Whoever they were, they were pretty bloody pathetic, cowards, sending a message like this. If it was meant to be a joke, it was a pretty cruel and unfunny one. No way was he going to let this note get to him.

Resisting the urge to tear the stupid thing into shred, he placed it with the other note in a desk drawer and tried to think through what he should do. Should he be alarmed? Was this a genuine threat of some obscure kind? Should he tell Julia? He knew she'd only worry.

In the days after he received the second note, he began to watch colleagues and his pupils with a keener eye, searching for any tell-tale signs of guilt - people whispering or smirking or laughing at him behind his back. One time when he walked past two pupils in a corridor they had laughed and he'd turned back and shouted at them, more aggressively than he'd intended. The two young boys had looked back at him, clearly shocked, tears in their eyes. But they hadn't been laughing at him, he soon discovered, and, after that, he told himself firmly that he mustn't let the notes unnerve him. It was stupid to obsess about the notes and he mustn't become paranoid.

The third note arrived at the end of the week. Same paper, same crude block capitals in the same black ink. This time it read, 'we're coming to get you'. Suddenly he felt dizzy and his heart was beating too fast. He stood up and steadied himself against the table. He had to sit back down again, the horrid note held in hands that, he noticed with alarm, were trembling uncontrollably. This wasn't something he could just put to one side and simply forget. Perhaps he should report it to senior management. Not sure, though, what they'd make it of it, or do. What did they mean, coming for him? Clearly this was one was a threat. This one was serious. He couldn't just brush this note off. But, could he really be in danger? Here, at school? If this note was from a colleague, it would be bullying of the worst kind.

Whoever had written the notes, he realised, must have had access to his room. And to his desk, either early in the morning or after most people had left school in the evening. He was definitely going to have to do something now. He should not have to put up with this. For the first time he was genuinely a little bit scared. In truth, more than a little bit scared.

Thinking about it afterwards, there may have been other clues. But he just hadn't put them together. There was a class he had been finding particularly difficult, for instance. An unruly lot, with a large, loud boy as their ringleader. He wasn't used to having discipline problems. An experienced, senior teacher, he had been at his present school a very long time. He was well liked and, usually, and respected. But this class were unsettled, troublesome and he had actually started to rather dread their lessons.

Then there was a year 11 class where he'd had to teach out of his subject specialism. The school were short of science teachers, as they often were, and so he'd had to mug up as best he could. And one boy had been manifestly unimpressed. Slumped over his work, headphones on, not doing anything, not going to do anything. When he'd confronted him after the lesson the boy slouched contemptuously in his chair.

'You don't seem to think I'm a very good Physics teacher,' he'd said.
'No, I don't,' the boy replied.
'Okay, fair enough,' he'd continued, keeping his tone as light as he could, 'but I really am trying my best to help you pass your GCSEs, so you might at least respond a little to that.'
'Yeah, mate, whatever, whatever you say.'

He'd given the boy a detention - for not doing his work and for his insolence. Really he'd wanted to hit him. That told him, if he didn't already know it, that his nerves were all jangled and he wasn't his usual, professional self. Perhaps this boy had written the notes. But that'd be odd. The notes had started before he'd taken over the class. Why

—

85

would the boy dislike him so much when he'd never taught him?

Soon after this incident he discovered the fourth and last note. The same paper, the same ink, the same writing. This time it read, 'look in your drawer, we've left something for you'. It must refer to one of his desk drawers, he realised quickly. Warily he opened each drawer in turn until he got to the bottom of the three, the largest drawer in which he kept spare files, paper, stationery and such like. And there it was, a shoebox, in plain, brownish grey cardboard. He stared at for a while and realised he was sweating. Eventually, carefully, using both hands he picked up the box. It was light, but there was something inside. He gave it a little shake. Whatever was inside slid lumpily from one side to the other. Taking a deep breath, he set the box down on his desk, wiped his hands on his trousers and opened the lid.

Inside the box was a small dead bird, just a fledgling. Its little head had been crushed. Jesus. And the smell, now the lid was off, it was disgusting, sweet and rancid. Quickly he stuck the lid back on. He'd have to take the dead bird out into the playground and dump in one of the big bins. He was halfway out of the classroom before he thought to take another picture first. It might be useful to have concrete evidence. He'd need if he was ever going to get whatever sick bastards who were doing this to him.

He was going to have to tell someone else about this now, certainly.

Only a few hours later, he was summoned to see the Head. A complaint had been made about him by an anonymous pupil, concerning his supposedly erratic recent behaviour. When he expressed bewilderment - nobody had ever complained about him before in a long, distinguished career - the Head had expressed sympathy, but been firm. Told him he needed to watch himself and conduct himself

—

professionally at all times, especially at this late stage in his career. Asked if he was feeling okay, whether everything was okay at home, with Juliet, and finally issued him an unofficial warning. Thanks for nothing, he thought. Should he have mentioned the notes and the dead rat? Maybe, but what would the Head have said or done anyway? He didn't want to give the man an excuse and he might have thought he was losing his mind. Perhaps he was.

The final move came when he received a text message from Julia during lunch break the following day to ring her immediately. Anxiously he did so straight away and waited, drumming his fingers on his desk, waiting for her to pick up the phone. It was a relief when he heard the familiar voice.

'There's a parcel,' she told him, 'arrived today in the post. And it needs signing for because it has 18+ contents, apparently.' Naturally Julia had been a bit taken aback. Had he, perhaps, been buying some kind of erotica? If so, it wasn't like him, not like him at all. But looking at the shape and size of the package she couldn't think of what else it could be. He knew it sounded paranoid, but he'd begged her not to open it, not until he got home. Perhaps that had just made him sound like he had something to hide, but reluctantly Julia had agreed. Get home as soon as you can, she'd said, because now she was really worried about him. He really hadn't seemed himself for weeks. Had there been any other developments? Perhaps he should tell her know about the other notes, and about the dead bird.

As soon as he got through the door, he'd torn open the package. Inside they discovered, with horror, a large hunting knife. Feverishly he searched for any message or any paperwork. But there was nothing other than the horribly serrated knife it its plastic packaging and an order confirmation with his name and address. No indication at all of

---

the sender. Immediately he contacted Amazon and when they'd said, sorry, they couldn't help, at Julia's insistence, he phoned the police.

A bored-sound officer had assured him that they'd certainly make enquiries and that he was to let them know if things escalated in any way. In what ways? he'd asked. Direct threats, actual violence, that sort of thing? He expected the police would do nothing, not until it was all too late.

What the hell's been going on? Julia had asked, holding his face between her hands and looking at him steadily in the eyes. He told her he didn't know, really, honestly, he had absolutely no idea. Had he done something he should tell her? It was okay, he could tell her anything. She loved him; she'd always love him. What was it? She could tell him. Oh Julia, Julia. He was so sorry that he'd broken violently away and screamed at her like that. But he'd been under so much strain lately, though it was no excuse. Really, she mustn't cry. Please, Julia, don't cry. He was so sorry. He was sorry about everything.

A couple of days after the knife had arrived and he was clearing his desk ready to go home for an extended period of rest and recuperation suggested by the SLT when something had made him look up from his piles of paperwork. And there they suddenly had been, standing in front of his desk, waiting silently and expectantly, standing perfectly still, looking straight at him. He must have been lost in his thoughts, because he hadn't heard them come in, had had no awareness of their presence until this very moment when he'd looked up. How long had they stood there? He had no idea.

A boy and a girl, two teenagers, probably year tens or thereabouts. Not pupils that he knew or had ever taught, certainly. A handsome boy with a head of close-cut blond hair, the girl's lustrous hair almost golden-coloured, arranged in long, criss-crossing plaits. Blue-eyed, perfect, unblemished pale skinned. Angelic looking teenagers, so unnervingly alike they must be twins. As he looked up, they stared evenly at him and held his gave for a while and then they both smiled.

'So. Now we've come to get you,' they had said in uncanny unison.

That had been the point at which he finally snapped.

Howl

'Hold on. Let me get this straight, you want to be allowed to wear a tail, to school, as part of your school uniform?' He tried and failed to keep the incredulity out of his voice. 'This might be a silly question, but why?' Pausing a moment, he added, 'and why on earth do you think we'd allow such a thing?'

The boy had asked to see the Deputy Head with a very special favour to ask. The Deputy Head knew the boy was indeed special, in various, sometimes rather alarming ways - that much had been clear from multiple reports from his teachers, and, in his time in the job, he'd heard some pretty strange requests. But this one really took the biscuit.

'Because it's my religious right to do so,' the boy replied evenly.

Studying the boy's composed expression, he wondered momentarily if this was, perhaps, some sort of prank. If it was, the boy was carrying it off with impressively cool style. Sitting across the desk, there in his seat, looking back at him levelly, he sounded entirely in earnest. Probably then he should take this request seriously, just to be on the safe side. 'Your religious right?' he said finally, weighing the words in his mouth. 'Sorry, I'm afraid you've lost me there. What religious rights are you referring to?'

The boy looked at him with mild surprise. Not even a flicker of embarrassment in the large grey eyes or any discernible sign of a suppressed smirk. 'Why, as an Otherkin, of course,' he said, raising one eyebrow slightly.

'An Otherkind?'

'No, an Otherkin. Without the 'd'. Specifically,' the boy cocked his head to one side, 'an Otherkin Furry. That's what I identify as.'

Okay, this conversation had started off badly, but now, it seemed, it was rapidly veering off into further weirdness. He decided to try to pull it back onto more familiar territory. 'Listen, Arthur, as you know, we expect Sixth Formers at TGS to wear suits. Even if we did allow it and I'm certainly not saying we ever would, I'm not sure how you could even fix a tail to a suit, putting aside the matter of why you'd want to.' He couldn't quite believe that he was saying this, but, nevertheless, he added, 'what sort of a tail are we talking about here?'

'A wolf's tail,' the boy replied, his large eyes staring across the table with an oddly limpid glaze. 'I just told you, I identify as an Otherkin Furry.'

There was no way around the topic. 'An Otherking Furry. Right. A wolf's tail. I see,' he said, nodding his head slightly. God give him strength. Surely this had to be some sort of stitch-up. Someone - other pupils or even a member of staff - must have put the boy up to this. Best thing to do would be to laugh and show he hadn't been taken in. But, on the other hand, if the boy was as serious as he seemed, the conversation might uncover some serious welfare issues. Perhaps Arthur was disturbed in some way. A wolf is predatory animal, after all.

'Okay, Arthur,' he leant forward on his desk, put his hands together as if in prayer and again looked the boy straight in the eye. Somehow he knew he might be opening a can of worms, but wasn't that part of his job? 'Perhaps you should tell me about being a Otherkind Fuzzy and what you call your religious beliefs...' He opened a drawer in his desk

---

and extracted a pen and some paper, 'would you mind if I made some notes?'

As he would recount to his wife later that night during dinner, the boy had told him he'd got interested in Otherkinness online, initially. He'd found forums in which interests in anthropomorphism were shared and discussed with the seriousness he felt they deserved. The boy had always known he was different, but it had taken a while for him to work out in exactly what ways. Initially shy, he had engaged online, before eventually, after many months of feverish activity, he'd been able to pluck up enough courage to attend a live convention. And it was there, at this very first one, that'd he'd made the breakthrough and discovered his true Otherkin Furry identity.

It turned out that the boy hadn't actually been born to the woman masquerading as his birth mother. He was, in fact, an Otherkind, created in some sort of astral dimension by the coupling of his spirit mother, who he believed to have been half-wolf, half-human with a polyamorous and powerful entity that intermittently manifested on earth in the form of a shaman. The boy admitted some of this revelation was rather confusing, that he was still processing it and that he wasn't 100% sure he had all right in his head, as his thoughts could get a bit foggy sometimes, but he knew in his bones it was true.

'My true origin,' the boy told him matter-of-factually, 'was revealed to me during a session of astral projection.' Right. That was something else he'd have to follow up at an opportune moment.

'Okay, I see. I've got all that. Thank you Arthur for being so candid and honest with me.' He looked up from his scribbled notes. Still the boy looked back at him levelly. 'And I presume you've attended more conferences since then, is that right?'

Matter-of-factually the boy told him how at another Otherkin convention he'd discovered his true sexual identity while dressed up as a wolf and that he was now in a loving long-term relationship with another Furry. Furries, it transpired, were a particular subspecies of Otherkins, ones who had wolf DNA coursing through their blood.

'Unlike other subspecies of Otherkins,' the boy continued, his voice a flat monotone, but his large glittering with sudden excitement, 'Furries, like me, have the power to pass on our wolfishness, through the transfer of pheromones.' He held the Deputy Head with his strange grey eyes, 'This only works, though, when others have the latent potential for Furriness'.

An oddball, no doubt, but the boy was a rather sweet, weedy, innocuous looking type. Nevertheless it was still alarming when he confided that he saw ordinary humans as others, as less evolved, inferior beings.

Once, finally, the boy had finished his story, he let him have the bad news. 'Sorry, Arthur. While I respect your Otherkingness, I'm going to have to turn down your request to wear a tail. School rules are there to be followed after all. If I allow this, it could be the thin end of the wedge. But, I promise we'll keep the situation under constant review and I will discuss your case with the Head, as soon as possible.'

The boy had listened attentively and seemed unfazed by his decision. He hadn't raised any objections. Just sat there, in his chair, staring back at him. But for the last few minutes, as his request had been turned down, the boy had been emitting a quiet growling sound.

'Okay, Arthur? I do hope you think I've been fair.'

Just a nod, and still the low growling.

'You're sure?'

'Yes,' the boy said and the growling stopped.

So, he'd told him he'd like to see him again at the same time next week and instructed the boy to book an appointment with his secretary. Next time there'd be the opportunity for more discussion, perhaps with some other key people involved. As he sent the boy off to his classes, he knew he'd have to pass on this most peculiar and disconcerting conversation to the Senior Team and also to the school's child welfare officers.

Of course, during his time in the job as Deputy Head he'd heard some pretty outlandish things. He lived in the South West, after all, and at least one local town was awash with all sorts of ridiculous mumbo-jumbo about white goddesses, moon cults, crystal healing, wizards and similar lunacy. But this Furry Otherkin thing, that was a new one on him.

Maybe it was an elaborate joke, after all. If it was a prank, it was a brilliant one and, he had to admit, the boy must be a genius actor. Yes, the whole story was so utterly absurd, so entirely ridiculous. A whole load of moonshine. Now that he thought about it, it smacked of a work of fantasy fiction – the tail, the otherkindness, the revelatory, 'origin story'.

Roughly grasping his cup between fingers, the nails of which he noticed were badly in need of a trim, grinning broadly to himself, he took a long slurp of his coffee, leant back in his chair and howled.

Much Ado about No Thing *or* Things Can Only Get Better

So, there was this thing okay that he wanted and the more that he thought about it the more that he wanted it. But, of course, he knew it was really horribly greedy of him to want something he didn't really need and that, it would be better if he saved his cash and waited for something bigger or more worthwhile to come along. Or, indeed, better still, to try to re-direct his energies away from accumulating any more things at all. Surely that would be a much better idea. Yes, that was his way and his light. That would be a much wiser course of action. He wasn't going to be sucked into cross commercialism. He didn't need the latest thing. Mindless consumption ruins the planet. But, on the other hand, it was a very nice thing. Very nice indeed.

Didn't he already know that any pleasure the thing would bring would only be short-lived? You're quite right there, buddy-o. The arrival of the thing, the opening of it, like he was a spoilt child at Christmas, the trying it on for size – jeez, was he still a child at heart? Then probably the doing with the thing the thing he most wanted to do it with it. So much marvellous thinginess, for sure, yes siree. For a little while. Total immersion in experiencing the thing. But, where was the point, the purpose, the beauty, or usefulness in the thing and in having the thing for himself, right? Come on, he had to confess that none of those things really pertained to the thing. Looking at it that way, and the thing really had no true depth or lasting value. It lacked majorly in the spiritual department. Really he was better off thingless.

Would it make him happier or make his life easier? Okay, maybe, it would for a while. Would it be of benefit to anyone else though? Well, fair enough, him and the thing was just pure selfishness, really. He knew

---

that. He'd admit to that. Maybe, just maybe others might benefit a tiny bit from his improved mood, possibly, at a stretch. But that wasn't why he wanted it and he knew it.

If he was really going to go all out to get this thing, then he'd have to shut up the annoying little man in his head, the little guy whose insistent voice nagged away at him, like his wife or his mother. 'Why do you need this thing? Don't you already have so many things already? Jeez, don't we've a whole house full of things already? Don't you care about using up all the world's resources? Don't you, you great big, selfish so-and-so.' No, it wasn't a man, it was more like a fat and sanctimonious insect, buzzing in his ear. An invisible, naggy, annoying wifey-sounding insect he couldn't see nor brush away or squash decisively flat with his hand.

But he/it/she told the truth, of course, really he couldn't deny it. He did have things everywhere, it was undeniably true, things of all shapes and sizes for all sorts of different purposes, stuffed into cupboards, bursting from drawers and hanging in wardrobes all around the house. Some of them, he still didn't know what they were for. But, then again, nothing quite like this particular thing. And this special thing, see, it would only be available for a very short time and if he didn't take the chance to seize it now, he'd never have the pleasure of possessing it. And that would be a little death to him. At least for a short while. Yes, he couldn't deny it, it might be selfish and shallow of him. No, right, correction: it was entirely selfish and shallow of him, but he really did want to have that thing. He really did. He had desire for that thing bad.

And, really any even vaguely fair-minded observer, even you, oh stony-faced one, would have to acknowledge, that this thing was a real, bona fide 100% bargain. Not only that, but it would only be on offer for a very short while. So you had to be quick and grab it through that window, before somebody else just went ahead and grabbed it first.

96

Could he afford it? What might be the consequences of getting it?

Okay. Good questions, my friend. Questions he can't in all good conscience swerve. He must definitely consider them before getting the thing. Or not getting it, of course. Because that was still an option, definitely. Yes, he had to confess, the cost was still high, despite the once-in-a-lifetime offer. But, on the other hand, didn't he work hard? Didn't he deserve some kind of reward for all of his hard labour? All of these long years of blood, sweat and toil? Yes, he did. And what was a life worth devoid of little rewards and pleasures? Not much, surely. He wasn't a monk after all. He wasn't a goddamn communist. He hadn't taken any vows of abstinence. Jeez, for God's sake. Didn't everybody like to get new things? Of course they did. That's how the world goes, doesn't it? Oh reason not the need, as the great man said. So come on, what's the big deal? What's your problem? Why you giving him such a hard time? You a saint or something? No? Then get down off that high horse of yours and cut him some slack, why don't you? Jeez. Some people.

Decisively he would shut out annoyingly persistent voices [like yours, which I'm sorry have to tell you is tiresomely self-righteous] and set about getting the thing and it wasn't really that hard to get, if he put his mind to getting it. Didn't even have to leave the house. How easy and convenient was that? Just a couple of clicks and it was his. Yes, he would get that thing and make sure too that when he got it, he maximum enjoyed it. Savoured every last bit of it. Got the absolute all the pleasure juice out of it. Sucked that goddamn thing bone dry. No sirree, he wouldn't waste a single thing of that thing. Wouldn't that be a kind of way of justifying it? Surely, you must agree.

Hold on though, would getting this thing mean that he didn't want another thing shortly after, perhaps even want it more than before? Oh, you really don't know when your beat, do you buddy? No, Listen

---

- wouldn't he soon want some other new special thing? Maybe getting the one would just whet his appetite for getting more. Jeez, he had to admit, that was possibly true. Very possible. Had been possibly true in the past. So. Oh, to hell with it all.

But, then again, on the other hand, that's true of food isn't it? We get hungry and then we eat something. We don't think, hold on, I've had this grumbly feeling in my stomach before, even though I ate something and it seemed to make it go away, but only for a little while, so I therefore conclude there's no point trying that eating thing again.

Heh, what do you want a man to do anyway, starve himself? Is that what you want? What kind of a friend are you anyway? I'm beginning to think you may have some kind of personable grudge against this poor guy. Do you think he'd strap on his moral high heels if you wanted to get a thing? I doubt it, I really do.

That's decided then. Settled. Finally. Once and for all. Just a couple of clicks and…

Goddammit, he was too late. Out of stock. Some other schmuck had got there first. Jeez, what an idiot he'd been for not being more decisive and FOR LISTENING TO YOU. And you, buddy, I hope you're feeling good about denying a man his thing. Bedevilling him with all your endless stupid questions. Well done you. Congratulations. I mean it. Some applause please. Pat yourself on the back, why don't you?

Blast and damnation. Hadn't he really, really liked that thing. And now he had no chance of getting it, ever.

Hold on a cotton-picking minute, though. What was that other thing, over there? That really does look fine. That thing's real nice. Now that thing, that looks like an even better bargain. He really needed that.

A Miracle

'Plates?'

What was it exactly in Miriam's voice that grated on him so?

'Why haven't you done the plates?' she went on, 'didn't I ask you to do the plates.'

That all-too-familiar, terse, irascible tone, of course. The way she was always bossing him about, like he was a stupid dog or a recalcitrant child - that too. She was smiling, apparently warmly, at him, in front of the guests, who were standing around awkwardly in the kitchen having only recently arrived. But it wasn't a friendly smile - that smile was a sort of warning; he knew that smile. Then Miriam turned her smile on the guests, as if to say, look what I have to put up with.

It was embarrassing to be talked to like this in front of other people, in front of guests. Being humiliated at home in private was bad enough, but in front of other people it was a form of torture. But, for the sake of the dinner party, he pulled an apologetic, goofy grin, raised his eyebrows in comic, put-upon fashion and bore it the best he could. He might sneak a conspiratorial look at Justin, shrugging it off, but, inside, he was already boiling.

'Yes, dear, of course, dear. Anything you say dear.'

Miriam shot him a warning look from over by the hob. 'It's not much to ask, is it, when I've been slaving away over dinner for the last hour and more.'

99

Their guests shifted uneasily on their feet, not knowing where to look.

'Once you've done the plates, would you like to see what our guests would like to drink?' Miriam prompted him helpfully.

Yes, of course, as if he wouldn't have thought to do that. He'd do the plates and then do the drinks. And then do Miriam, if she wasn't careful.

✻

'You ought to take up cycling,' Miriam was informing him across the dinner table after having a long conversation with one of the guests, the extraordinarily dull and vapid, Simon, 'it would help you get rid of that paunch of yours.' Miriam seemed to find that wildly funny, insulting him and his middle-aged body like that, in front of everyone, vaunting her contempt for his feelings. Simon was laughing too, although a little more nervously. With good reason. Kevin and Annie were both smirking. Miriam'd been drinking steadily, of course, all evening and seemed, at times like these, to get some sort of perverse kick from humiliating him. 'Simon's got all the equipment. And he knows lots of great routes around here, don't you Simon. Why don't you two get together for a ride?'

Good God, he'd rather boil his head in a bucket of acid. He had nothing against vapid Simon, of course, not really, apart from his spectacular vapidity. But he couldn't really bare his loud and horsey wife, Geraldine. But the couple were Miriam's friends and so he tolerated their company at the occasional dinner party. If you diluted them with some more interesting and less needy people, they could be perfectly tolerable, almost, if he didn't have to see them too often. Or talk to them much.

Of course, he was obliged to respond. Everyone was looking eagerly at him. 'Yes, maybe. As no doubt Miriam will tell you, my equipment's probably not as impressive as yours, Simon. And, anyway, I'm trying to keep going with the running...'

'You can do both, you know, Michael,' Miriam fired back, 'it'll help get some of that weight off.'

'Easier too on the knees,' Justin chipped in, 'My knees are terrible these days. And running's terrible for knees.'

Fortunately, Simon didn't seem much keener than him on the idea of joint bike rides, though it was hard to tell with Simon. The man's greatest enthusiasms never rose much above the level of tepid.

Thankfully, Miriam turned her attention to Justin and the topic of bad knees. They always flirted a little together, those two. Really, it was all rather embarrassing. But Justin's rather youthful and attractive wife, Isabelle, never seemed to mind, and so Michael also let it go.

It hadn't always been like this with Miriam. They were just going through one of those occasional dips in their marriage. Over ten years they'd been married, or more, and they stumbled into these rough patches from time to time. Didn't that happen to everyone? He expected so. Physically during these dips they touched less, kissed infrequently and then grew almost physically awkward with each other. Just the odd perfunctory peck at the start of the day and before turning over and going to sleep at night. But even this current state of hostility could be changed by something out-of-the-blue. While Michael's moods tended to sit heavily on him for hours at a time, Miriam could swing wildly from fury to tenderness in minutes. And just as swiftly back again.

'Can you please offer our guests another drink?' Miriam was addressing him again in that regal way of hers. 'Did you put another bottle of that nice white in the fridge, like I asked you to?' Again she tilted her head at him, as if he were a dog, 'Did you manage to remember to do that, for me, Michael?'

'Yes, of course, dear.' He met her smile with an equally cold one.

'Well, would you like to run along and get it then?' Miriam surveyed the table grandly, 'If we have to wait for you offer another drink we'll all die of thirst first…'

'I'm on my way already,' he said, rising gratefully from his chair.

❋

As he half-listened to vapid Simon droning on about his cycling equipment, nodding his head from time to time and throwing in the odd desultory comment, Michael watched his wife laughing and smiling with the other guests, charming them with her bright-eyed vivacity. She may have put on a bit of weight again, but she could be vivacious, Miriam, it was one of things that had first attracted him to her, that vivacity. In company, especially after a drink or two, she was a woman transformed. Rarely had she seemed so brightly alive with him over the last two weeks, two weeks of continual simmering, uneasy tension.

Now she was telling still-very-pretty Isabelle, all about his latest travails in the History department. If Miriam had overheard him disparaging her parents earlier, she showed no sign of it. Justin had laughed along uneasily as Michael had once again made merry about his in-laws' appallingly philistine tastes, though he had also glanced a couple of times in Miriam's direction. But Miriam was too engrossed in her own voluble conversations to take any notice of her husband. With a captive audience, she rarely bothered to listen to anything Michael had to say.

He gathered that Justin, clever and confident Justin, had been promoted, again - he did something complicated to do with health insurance, involving complex calculations of risk. It wasn't the sort of thing that interested Michael much and although Justin had tried to explain what he did several times, he hadn't really listened. Not that he begrudged Justin his career success. Justin might be a little smug, but he rather liked the man. Justin didn't try to be something he wasn't and he didn't suffer fools lightly. And he seemed to have the perfect marriage. And he was wealthy, self-confident and had a sharp sense of humour. Certainly he was better company than needy Geraldine, with all her loud, apparently cast-iron opinions or vapid Simon and his wan enthusiasms. Even if Justin did flirt a little too openly with his Miriam.

'Talking about me again, dear,' boldly he interrupted his wife mid-flow. 'Next you'll be calling me Swampy. Anyone need a top-up of wine?' he added, sweeping the guests with a genial smile.

'What?' Miriam sounded genuinely annoyed. There was a dangerously broken edge to her voice as she added, 'Sorry, Michael, what are you talking about?'

'He said you'll be calling him Swampy,' Geraldine clarified helpfully for everyone's benefit. 'Whatever that means.'

'What is that, some sort of supposedly clever literary illusion?' Miriam wasn't smiling at him now. Decisively she put down her glass and cocked her head at him. 'Is that meant to be amusing somehow, Swampy? Are you being witty? Was that one of your famous quips? If so, do please let us all in on the joke, so we know when to laugh.'

'Allusion, it's an allusion,' he said triumphantly, pushing his glasses back into place. 'Would you like some more?' He rose from his chair to pour wine into his wife's glass.

'No, thanks, I've had more than enough already,' Miriam said placing a protective hand over the top of the glass.

Michael turned to the guests, 'Justin, Simon, a top-up of wine? Kevin, perhaps another beer? Not an 'illusion', Miriam, an 'allusion'.

'What a great big pedant,' Miriam said and laughed. Following her lead, everyone else laughed too. 'It was just a slip of the tongue.'

But he'd embarrassed her, he knew it. He'd scored a hit, a palpable hit.

Picking up her glass and draining the remainder, Miriam guffawed again, 'Isn't my ill-equipped husband, a terrible old pendant? Oh my God, what a tedious, ill-equipped, old pedant!'

✳

Michael was doing the washing up. The guests had finished their cups of coffee and gone off into the night. As Justin had left, he'd given Michael a hearty slap on the back and said he'd seen him soon, he hoped, and then shook his hand. Geraldine had reminded him and Simon about getting together for a cycle ride. Kevin was invited too. Isabelle had given Miriam an overlong hug. Yes, yes, bye bye everyone. Safe journeys home etc. etc..

Now Miriam was noisily moving things about in the dishwasher where, earlier, he had stacked the dirty plates and bowls.

'Can people not even manage to put things in the dishwasher right.' Miriam bent over the machine and tutted loudly, 'How many times have I told you that things won't wash properly if they're placed like this? For Godssakes.'

Carefully he picked the carving knife out of the soapy water. So sharp, such a pointed blade; it really could do an awful lot of damage, if one wasn't careful, very careful.

'Can't you put things in the dishwasher so that they'll wash properly,' Evidently Miriam hadn't exhausted this topic yet, it seemed.

'What are we going to do with you, hey?' Her tone changed, suddenly softening. 'Sorry if I was horrible to you tonight, love, it's just the stress,' she added, putting her arms around his waist and squeezing, 'What with mum's fall and the work and everything. I know you have an awful lot to put up with, I really do. Mikey?' She kissed him gently on the back of the neck, once, twice. 'Mikey, I'm sorry.' She squeezed again.

'Mind you, you gave as good as you got, as usual.' He turned around then to face her. 'You know, Isabelle was really impressed by the news of your new book.' She was smiling at him now. And when she reached up and embraced him, he felt the first stirrings of lust. Miriam pulled back to look him fully in the face. She was smiling, tears in her bright, beautiful eyes. He kissed her then. Behind his back, clutched in his hand, the cool handle of the carving knife.

'It's a miracle, Mikey. An absolute miracle,' she said. 'I've checked and doublechecked again.' Miriam smiled at him. 'Didn't you notice that I

---

wasn't drinking tonight? Mikey I'm pregnant, We're going to have a baby.'

War and Peas

It is early in the morning when he enters the kitchen. The wife's already been up a couple of hours, working, no doubt. He hears her on the phone in the study to her boss. When she comes into the kitchen, she is crying a little.

'What's the matter?' he asks as puts the kettle on.
''You KNOW what's the matter,' she fires straight back at him.
'Sorry, I was only expressing concern…'
'No, you weren't. You know exactly what's the matter,' she says as she butters some toast and throws the dirty knife into the sink, 'I've had a terrible headache for weeks, I'm drowning in work and on top of it all, I can't sleep.'
'I'm sorry…' he tries again, feebly.
'No you're not.' She makes for the door.
'Alright then, I won't bother to ask in future,' he says angrily now, as he pours boiling water into his cup.
'Good, then, don't.'
'Good, then. Watch me, I won't.'

❋

Carefully he opens the door to the garden room where she is just about to finish her evening yoga session. He has cooked them a delicious dinner and it's almost ready to serve.

His wife is lying prostate on the floor on a yoga mat in her sports kit, eyes closed, her arms down by her sides, her hands with their palms up. Drifting in the background there's gentle, elevator style music. Issy is breathing gently. In and out. In and out. She looks like she might be asleep. There's a contented, dreamy smile on her face as if she is dreaming of summer holidays, of endless days lolling around on warm tropical beaches.

'Issy?' he ventures, sotto voce.

'What the FUCK?' Immediately Issy sits up and turns to stare at him, 'Can't you see I'm doing my FUCKING yoga in here?'

'Sorry…'

'I was all nice and relaxed and now you've gone and FUCKING RUINED it.'

'Sorry,' he says, slowly backing out of the room, 'so sorry.'

✳

'CAN'T YOU SEE, I'M TRYING TO WATCH THE TELE,' he shouts from the sofa.
'YES, WELL, I'M TRYING TO DO THE HOOVERING,' she shouts back.
'CAN'T YOU DO IT LATER?'
'NO. IT NEEDS DOING NOW.'
'FOR GOD'S SAKE, I'LL DO IT LATER,' he shouts. 'I'M TRYING TO WATCH THE TENNIS.'
'SOME PEOPLE HAVEN'T TIME TO WATCH THE TENNIS,' she shouts, 'CAN'T YOU SEE THE WHOLE HOUSE NEEDS CLEANING?'
'FOR GOD'S SAKE, I SAID, I'LL DO IT LATER.'
'YEAH, RIGHT.'
'TURN THAT BLOODY THING OFF, WILL YOU? I PROMISE.'

Kathryn is working on her dissertation at the dinner table. She has to work there because Issy is using the office and he is doing his best with the sitting room. It's lunchtime, but Kathryn's already had something, so he has to chop up the vegetables and put the sausage rolls in the oven as quietly as possible. He must not disturb his daughter's rapt concentration.

Earlier he overheard a heated conversation between his wife and daughter about various knotty issues with her dissertation, so he needs to be especially careful not to upset the apple cart now. He knows he is treading on eggshells. That there are emotional tripwires everywhere. He mustn't stumble clumsily onto a landmine.

'Would you mind if I listened to the radio, just while I'm eating?' he asks tentatively.

'For GODSAKES, dad, can't you see I'm TRYING to WORK in here?' Kathryn frowns and snaps at him, 'How the HELL am I supposed to concentrate with you BANGING around the place?'

'That's really not fair,' he retorts, sounding even to himself like a sullen teenager, 'I was being as quiet as possible. And anyway I need to have some lunch.'

Kathryn's frown grows thunderous. Now she throws her arms up in the air. 'That's SO SELFISH. I'm trying to WORK and you KNOW there's NOWHERE else I can go.'

'So you expect me to just sit in silence eating my lunch on my own?'

'YES! Why not? Is it really TOO much to ask, dad, IS it, really?'

'Well...'

'Right, okay, HAVE it your way,' Kathryn gets up from the table, picks up her laptop, sweeps up her papers and books and strides towards the kitchen door.

'Hold on,' he says as he turns on the radio, 'that's just not very reasonable.'

'Sure, dad.' Kathryn stands at the doorway. 'Couldn't you just be sympathetic, for ONCE in your life?' she calls as a parting shot as she slams the door hard behind her.

✴

'Have you seen these clothes?' Issy asks, laughing, as she flicks through the Sunday supplement at the breakfast table, 'I mean they're so utterly ridiculous. Take a look.' She pushes the open pages to his side of the table and laughs.

No, he's really not interested and, anyway, he's trying to read this article by a doctor on an oncology ward. And he wants to read the article about bucket lists next.

'Hey, go on, take a look at that,' Issy persists.

Before him is a long feature about a distinguished actress, accompanied by some fashion style glossy photos. The actress, who must be pushing on seventy, is got up in the most extraordinary street-style fashions - skin-tight bodices, pointy bras, huge ballooning pleated trousers, massive purple bovver boots.

'Ridiculous,' he concurs, 'and for a woman of her age.'

'WHAT?' Issy looks up at him from the newspaper she's been perusing and glares at him, her nostrils flaring.

'What do you mean 'a woman of her age'? What the HELL has her age go to do with anything?'

He is a little taken aback by her sudden fierceness. 'Well, I just thought the clothes, they look more like something a teenager might wear, and on her they seem...'

'WHAT? Hold on,' Issy is rising abruptly from her chair, 'hold on, are you saying she can't wear exactly what she likes BECAUSE OF HER AGE?'

'Well, I, err...'

'That,' Issy bangs her coffee cup down hard on the table, 'that is such a typical male prejudice. That is so chauvinist. REALLY I can't believe you said that!'

'What? What do you mean?'

'Well, you wouldn't say that about a man, would you? You wouldn't say that about a man.'

'What?' He is getting angry too now, feeling he has been wrongly accused, unfairly labelled as being a prejudiced old chauvinist. He raises his voice to match his wife's, 'Of course I would. Don't be so ridiculous Issy!'

'How DARE you call me RIDICULOUS?' His wife's body is quivering violently with rage now and her lips are pursed in that way she has when she's really furious, as if she is sucking on something horribly sour or scaldingly hot. 'How DARE you call me ridiculous!' she spits.

'You ARE being ridiculous.' He's not backing down now. It's too late for that. 'If you're saying I'm prejudiced!'

Issy's hands have curled into fists and it seems to be taking all her will to keep her arms down by her sides. 'Don't SHOUT at me Justin. Don't you DARE shout at me!'

'I am NOT shouting at you!' he shouts at her.

'YES YOU FUCKING ARE!!' she shouts back, squaring up to him across the table.

He's not having this. He gets up to leave the room. Over his shoulder, bravely or foolishly he fires a parting shot, 'You're such a hypocrite Issy. Such a bloody hypocrite!'

✳

'Not now, can't you see I'm up to my neck in it? At this rate I won't be finished 'til gone midnight.'

He stands indecisively in the doorway of the study. 'Okay, love, it's just that there's something…'

She picks up the phone, turns back to her screen. 'Yeah, yeah, whatever. No problem.' She's shooing him away with the other hand. 'We'll speak once I've finished Justin. Okay love?'

Later. Yeah. Whatever.

'Okay.'

112

Lux in Tenebris

When, out of nowhere, the window appears and opens up suddenly and unexpectedly, he only hesitates for a moment before leaping through and suddenly, unexpectedly he finds himself falling through the unexpected air until the unexpected ground rises suddenly to meet him, like the unexpected fist of God.

Touched

O

The

car door,

the steering

wheel, the traffic butt-

on and the door handle, the stair

rail and the classroom door, the light switch, the window frame

the pencil, pen and cup. The mouse, the keyboard, the table and the swivel chair. On our

faces, on our skin, in our lungs, everywhere the air was

touched.

Does not Computing

'Hello, sir. I am sorry for calling you today and I hope you are having a very nice good day. My name is Kevin and I am ringing you today because we have being detecting some suspicious irregularities in the use of your internet connection over night from your household...'

'Really? Sorry, you're ringing me from where exactly?'

'Indeed sir, I am ringing from our company head offices because we have detected some serious irregularities and you are needing to act quickly, sir, or your internet security will be at severe risk of being compromised.'

'Irregular use of our internet connection? And you're ringing me from where, India?'

'Indeed, that is right, sir. Suspicious and most irregular usage. Some sort of malware has probably been downloaded onto your laptop. That is most probable explanation, sir.'

'Right, I see, thank you, Kevin. That does sound very alarming. What do you recommend I do?'

'That is what we are ringing you all about sir...you will be needing to give us remote access to your computer to allow us to fix the problem...'

'Which company did you say you work for, Kevin?'

'I am ringing you today, sir, from your provider's customer services department because this situation has now been marked as most urgent and for immediate action.'

'That's kind of you, Kevin. Hold on a second though, Kevin from India, another much bigger problem has suddenly cropped up. Oh Jesus! Go away! GO AWAY'

'What is it, sir?'

'You won't believe this, Kevin, but an elephant is right now taking a huge dump in my front garden.'

'An elephant, sir? Did you say an elephant?''

'Yes, an elephant Kevin. And in Basingstoke, of all places. Dumping right in the middle of my garden. On my lovely front lawn. The cheeky so-and-so. Oh that's a huge pile of turdage, Kevin, it really is. Can you believe it Kevin? I can see the great big pink brute now from my study window... Really butter wouldn't melt. Get off with you. Go away, you great pink, hairy brute.'

'Go away Sir?'

'Not you, Kevin from India, the elephant. I'm trying to shoo it away now through the study window. Hold on a second, Kevin. I'm going to have to go outside and try to frighten it off with a brolly. Hold on. Won't be a minute...'

'Yes, indeed, sir, I will hold on. But...'

※

'Sorry for keeping you so very long, Kevin from India, but I'm afraid the elephant's taking absolutely no notice of my attempts to shoo it away. Kevin, I have to tell you, it's easily the biggest elephant I've ever seen, in the whole of Basingstoke. A monster. Perhaps I should call the police or the zoo. Or the perhaps the high commissioner? What do you think Kevin? So sorry for dragging you into this huge pink elephant emergency Kevin, but I really desperately need your help and you're a customer services something or other...'

'That is no problem at all sir, but...'

'Do you think, Kevin that someone at my provider's customer services department headquarters in India who's been monitoring my internet connection overnight and find a most alarming something or other and so needs direct access to my computer might be able to help me. With the elephant fiasco, I mean? Could you ask your supervisor. Better still,

116

maybe, you could send someone round to take a look?'

'I am very sorry sir, but...'

'Kevin, please. Help me Kevin? I need help urgently. Kevin, I'm getting down right now on my hands and knees to pray to the Good Lord for your help. Please Kevin. If you like I can give you direct access to the elephant. Might that possibly help? Hold on a moment - I'll take the phone outside and put you into direct contact. Just wait one moment...'

'I am sorry sir, but I can only be helping you with the problem with your internet, sir, not about any elephants...'

'Yes, but Kevin, if you had an elephant dumping copiously in your front garden in a little bungalow in a small village just outside Basingstoke, on the lawn you've carefully cultivated over many years, wouldn't you think that was the main problem you had to deal with? Your most pressingly immediate concern Kevin? Wouldn't that be what your training as a customer services support person tells you?'

'I am not understanding, sir. About the elephants. As I am saying, sir, I am ringing about a most urgent issue with your internet connection.'

'Jesus, I don't believe it! Kevin!'

'What is it, sir. Are you still there? Sir? Sir?''

'Sorry, Kevin, a call's just come in from my long-lost Nigerian cousin's mobile... It's HMC, Revenue and Customers. You won't believe this, Kevin, but there's a tax fraud case and if I don't press number 1 immediately and enter my bank details, I'm in danger of being arrested and carted off down to the courthouse... Jesus! Kevin, please, can you help? Kevin? Are you still there Kevin? Kevin?'

Upside Down Pudding

Justin pushes the last morsels of food around his plate indecisively with his fork. He'd begun eating with real gusto, but the portions at this fancy new restaurant are surprisingly large and he is starting to regret having that cold beer with the starter. Taking a sip from the ridiculously overpriced wine, he looks up at the beautiful young woman opposite him and smiles at her, a little self-consciously.

At the start of the year Justin had decided that he didn't have enough sex in his life. Nearly in his fifties now, still relatively fit, he figured that, realistically, there was a limit to how much more sex he was likely to have during the rest of his days on this earth, which, after all, were numbered. He didn't believe in God, heaven or any kind of afterlife, but even if he did wake after death and, presuming he made it upstairs, he doubted that there'd be much sex in that ethereal realm either.

Slim and still youthful looking, his wife, Issy, was certainly an attractive woman, even to his somewhat jaded eyes. Just ask any of his male friends. Ask Michael for one. But she parcelled out their marital sexual delights these days with all the relish of a miser throwing pennies at the poor and needy. And Justin was certainly in need.

If he was in luck, they might have it once a month. Usually on a Saturday night, their physical self-consciousness eased and their awkward passions lubricated by alcohol. Habitually Issy prefers the light to remain firmly off these days, which he finds a little insulting. But he dares not say anything. The problem, though, is not the quality of the sex, it is the tiny, spartan portions.

The restaurant is a pretty swanky place, a cut above the sort of establishment he habitually frequents. Plush décor, comically snooty waiters, an impressively fancy wine list, that sort of place. Justin doesn't mind the prices - he can afford them. And, after all, you can't take it with you, as his later father always said. And the old bastard had been true to his word.

He'd heard about this place from the chaps at the tennis club and had long been keen to give it a try. Plus, it is tucked away out in the sticks, discretely out-of-town. And now he has found the perfect excuse to give it a go. He takes another sip from his wine. He has to admit, it is very nice - full-bodied, with both subtlety and depth, just the way he likes it.

From time to time, the thought of hiring a prostitute has flitted through Justin's sex-starved mind. In these over-heated, lurid moments, he assures himself that there are such things as high-class prostitutes who really are not being exploited by their wealthy clients. If anything, it is the other way round, surely. Now that the children have grown-up and are living away from home, with their own separate lives, there might be opportunities for this sort of illicit sexual liaison, perhaps. And if not now, then when? It would provide a much-needed thrill in his erstwhile dully predictable life. Occasionally Issy's work requires her to be away for the odd night, sometimes even a whole weekend. He has both motive and opportunity.

But, what would happen if a nosy neighbour saw something? An unfamiliar young woman arriving at his doorstep, possibly in a fur coat – did they really wear them? - while his wife is away for the weekend. A young woman ushered furtively into the house before emerging an hour or so later. A highly respectable member of the community, he is a governor at the local primary school, a veritable pillar of local society.

119

The risk might be exciting, but the scandal would ruin him.

Moreover, fundamentally Justin believes himself to be a decent guy, at least as moral as the next chap. In his heart of hearts, he knows prostitution is a vile, exploitative business, whatever anyone says to the contrary, and, in reality, he wants nothing to do with something so sordid. Plus, the thought of how it'd devastate Issy, if ever she found out, that is too ghastly to contemplate. He might want more sex, but he still loves his wife, at least 75% of the time. The cost benefit analysis just doesn't look good. Still, a man has his needs.

As he finishes his last mouthful of deliciously tender beef, moistened by a lovely, delicate jus, he wonders whether, he might just be able to squeeze in a sweet after all. There are the calories to consider, of course. But wasn't he has been a regular runner, despite two dodgy knees?

Justin's needs were growing increasingly desperate. Time, after all, was running out. Naturally, there was always porn. These days it was all-too-easy to access the stuff via the internet. It was the subject of light-hearted, nudge-nudge jokes among male friends and colleagues and he wasn't above looking at the odd topless snap of an attractive model when it happened across his attention, from time to time. But, what about the dreaded electronic footprint? What might be revealed by too close inspection of his late-night internet searches? If he was honest with himself, though he'd seen precious little of it, he found the so-called 'harder' stuff more of a turn-off than a turn-on - in fact, in truth, he found it crass and demeaning. For both parties. Even the softer stuff made him feel, afterwards, dirty and ashamed. He was a better man than this, surely.

In normal circumstances, he calculates he would burn the weight of the average pudding off with a couple of moderate runs. If he could still run. But, another factor to consider is that he doesn't want to appear gluttonous. Probably the best thing is to ask if she would like a sweet and go along with that.

What options were left? How in all good conscience could he have more sex without comprising himself or his marriage? A few months back there'd be a little frisson with one of his best friend's wives, the famously vivacious Miri. A drunken moment of intimacy in the back garden during a particularly boozy Christmas party. But the moment had passed, and nothing had ever come of it, which in all truth, was a relief to both of them. Michael was a friend.

He has to say, the music is particularly well-judged; atmospheric and not so loud that you can't hold a conservation, not that they were talking much. He wouldn't normally listen to free-form jazz - it is too shapeless for his tastes. But this stuff, whatever it, is pleasantly light and melodic. It has a definite feel-good vibe. It makes him feel good, his thoughts drifting along with it. Should he order a sweet? No, on balance, he doesn't think so.

Of course, he's tried in the past to broach the subject with Issy. But she never listens. Quickly she becomes prickly and defensive and shuts the conversation down. The thought of suggesting some sort of 'open' arrangement is too ludicrous to even countenance. He doesn't want her to storm out of the house in horror. At his age, and especially now, he doesn't want to find himself divorced and all alone.

Nevertheless, when the new girl started at Head Office Justin's imagination had begun to expand in feverish directions. She wasn't just pretty, this young woman, she was truly, breath-takingly beautiful. Dark-haired, dark-eyed, sultry-looking, like a Spanish princess in a fairy tale. And it almost made Justin blush even to think about her body. So slender and lithe and so full of life. But the really remarkable thing about this extraordinarily beautiful young woman was that she seemed to find Justin attractive, even at his advanced age.

At first, he told himself that he must be mistaken. Told himself to get a grip on his overactive imagination. Told himself that If he wasn't careful, he could make a terrible fool of himself here. All those smiles? She was being friendly. Naturally, she was just trying to make a good impression at the start of her career. He was simply misreading the signals. Perhaps it was an age thing; she couldn't be much older than his daughter. That tilt of the head and he must be imagining it, the slight pouting of her lips, as he tried to give her some instructions about a client, that couldn't be flirtatious, could it? Not really, no.

The young woman opposite him is telling him now about her work. An important project. She is very animated, passionate even. He admires that. Half-listening to her, half-listening to the music, he watches closely, and nods or shakes his head and drops in the occasional supportive comment at opportune moments. She really is so beautiful, vibrant, so very alive. She reminds him of his wife, Issy, when she was a young woman. Perhaps he is still a little hungry.

Emotionally, he isn't a complete cretin. Nor so long in the tooth. The way his new junior colleague began to look back at him when he found himself looking at her. Staring at her, in fact. The way she smiled back at him. Perhaps she saw him as some kind of meal ticket for her career. Calculated the advantages. Weighed the pros and cons. Well, so what? If their relationship benefitted both of them, then why the hell not?

How many times did this sort of opportunity crop up in one's life? What was he anyway, a man or a mouse? Aren't the things we most regret, those rare opportunities we didn't seize with oh so grateful hands. Carpe diem, and all that. If not now, then when? Never, that's when. Because think of the consequences.

Upside down pudding, with crème anglais. Surprising to find that on the menu at a fancy restaurant. He hadn't seen that on a menu for, must be, donkeys' years. His mother used to make it back in the seventies and eighties. He'd really loved upside down pudding, especially with custard. Hadn't had it for decades. Issy had never liked it.

He'd put the conversation they had to have off for as long as was possible. Just tried to live in these precious, magical moments. Enjoy being out at this fancy restaurant, eating good food, drinking great, albeit overpriced wine, half-listening to the easy, feel-good music, enjoying the company. He hadn't felt this good in a long time. He didn't want to break the spell.

But, he knows the enchantment can't last forever. Knows he needs to pluck up his courage and, somehow, to find the right words.

'Listen, sweetheart,' he says finally, reaching over and taking one of her lovely slender hands in his, 'you're probably wondering why I've brought you here.' He takes a long, deep sip of his wine and places the glass down decisively. 'Well, I've something to tell you and I want you to promise me you won't tell anyone else.' He squeezes her hand in his. 'Promise me, this will be our secret, just between us. That no one else knows. For now, at least.' He waits for her to nod her head before continuing. 'Okay, sweetheart.' He tries to smile. 'The results came back this week. And they're bad, very bad. The worst possible in fact.' He finds, as he looks up and the door to the restaurant opens, that suddenly, there are tears in his eyes. But despite himself, he is smiling.

'I want you to promise me, sweetheart,' he says smiling, 'that you won't say anything to anyone, not even to your mother.'

The Last Reports

What is often called 'lively' in the classroom, i.e. a loud, lippy, disruptive yobbo with only a primitive appreciation of the value of education and, for that matter, for personal hygiene.

Shows bags of enthusiasm. Unmatched by any semblance of talent.

Frankly, not sure who this is. So faceless and innocuous, in two years hardly registered on anyone's consciousness. Nice enough, probably. Punctuality probably good.

Possibly more suited to practical subjects.

Far too clever for own good. Parents Oxford-types. Insufferably smug. Blue Stocking in the making. Spectacularly plain and dumpy, thank God. No doubt hopeless at sports. Probably records teacher errors in a big black book.

So covered in volcanic spots and explosive pustules one really doesn't like to get too close. Enjoys reading out loud. Generally does so badly.

Meek, God-botherer. Wholesome, but unappetising, like bran flakes. Girl Guide? Oversized feet.

Bright, sensitive soul. Always immaculate presentation. Probably bats for other side.

Complete neanderthal, blissfully unaware of this fact. Unafraid to broadcast ignorant and asinine opinions on a wide range of topics. Suit the army. Infantry division.

15 going on 50. Dull as proverbial ditch water. Good with numbers, apparently. Stellar career in accountancy awaits.

Thinks he's the cool kid in class. Isn't.

Quite extraordinary cleavage, about which terribly embarrassed. Future hubby unlikely to mind.

More sense of rhythm than any other type of sense. Doesn't settle to academy study. Probably good at dancing and/or sport.

Lacks any semblance of grace, culture or refinement. Popular with the older boys.

Arrogant little shit. Thinks he knows more than the teacher. Sometimes does. The little shit.

Morbidly obese. Flabbiness not just confined to physicality. Weight appears to exert considerable gravitational pull on frankly miniscule brain. Runs in the family. Voice like a foghorn.

Makes a sloth look excited and zippy. Monumentally inert, except for being somewhat gaseous.

Would have been locked up or exhibited by the Victorians. Genuinely unhinged. Scary.

One of two indistinguishable Chinese boys. Very quiet, as their type tend to be. Polite. Finds mastering use of auxiliary verb and expressing own opinions insurmountable challenges.

Beguilingly pretty. Something of the young Bardot. Honey-blond hair freckly-faced, bee-kissed lips, shapely. Will grow up to be an absolute stunner.

Adds nothing to the sum total of human happiness. Given the opportunity may well, in time, actively reduce it. Worryingly good with hands.

Dungarees, etc. Something of a Feminazi. Walks up the wrong side of the road. Probably not by choice.

Sycophantic little creep. Expect enjoys torturing insects in private. Political career beckons. Or, possibly, serial killer.

Face liked a wiped arse. Joyless. Zero sense of humour. Time will turn her into a politically correct harridan, like obnoxiously woke mother.

The other Chinese boy. See earlier report.

Untrustworthy, devious little monster. Zero sense of social responsibility. Will go far.

Quiet Indian or perhaps Pakistani boy. Hard-working. Good at cricket?

Mouth like a whore. Probably gives boyfriends, plural, tremendous b-js.

✴

Hacking the school reporting system turned out to be a simple affair.

Covering their tracks shouldn't be too hard either, they reckoned. And old Horny Crotch was such a complete wanker, it was well worth the risk. How richly he deserved this parting gift, for his long-anticipated retirement.

That should do it nicely, she thought and, uttering a quick prayer, pressed 'submit'.

Deal or no Deal

Listen, how long have we known each other?

Why, since primary school, donkeys years. why do you ask?

Because, I want to ask you a favour

Okay, go on

A big favour

Right

A really big favour

Go on, I'm all ears

Okay, as you know, times are hard, really hard and we all need to be enterprising to try to make ends meet

Sure do

There's little work out there because the economy's screwed, so we have to be resourceful

Truth

So, well, I have a sort of proposal for you

Alright, go on. I'm all ears

Okay, I want you to loan me your husband

You want what?

I want you to loan me your husband. I want you to loan me Kevin. Only for a little while

You want to loan Kevin?

That's right. That's it

I don't understand. What are you talking about?

Alright, just hear me out. Let's say you come to an estimation of Kevin's annual worth to you as a husband. Obviously there's the money he brings in from the job. Add to that other things he does of worth to or for you – vis-à-vis maintaining the house, mowing the lawn, sorting the paperwork for the car, that sort of thing

Okay...

Add to that, any other services he might provide. Obviously there's the companionship, that must be worth something, plus maybe a bit of entertainment value...

We're talking about my Kevin? Entertainment value?

And, then, there are those other things that a husband and a wife, you know...

You're pulling my leg

No, surely that's a service provided, isn't it?

Well, I've never thought of it like that. Hold on a minute, in that case, aren't I the one providing that particular service?

Well, suppose so. Depends. I'd say you both are. But I'm only interested in the value to you. Over the course of a year

A year?

Right. How much?

For that? Let's just say we're not talking big bucks here. Or big anything, for that matter

Okay. Right. I see. But add that to all the other value Kevin provides each year and you've got your husband's net worth. And I propose to pay you half of that, as a loan

Half of it? As a loan?

Sure

Is this some kind of sick joke?

No. I'm deadly serious, honest Indian. I want you to loan me your husband. Just for a short while

Listen, I know you've had it a bit rough recently, what with the divorce and everything, but this is just crazy talk. You can't be that desperate, surely. My Kevin?

Your Kevin. And now, here's the real beauty of the thing. At the end of the loan period, as agreed between the two parties, that's vis-à-vis you and me, I'd sell you back your Kevin at half the price of his worth

———

130

Hold on, what do you mean? I loan him to you and then you sell him back to me?

That's right, for half his worth. Say you valued Kevin at, I don't know, 50k a year

50k? Kevin? My Kevin?

Okay, let's say 30k. I pay you 15k for you to lend me Kevin and then you pay me 15k at the end of the loan period to buy him back again; in effect I'm selling Kevin back to you

But you only loaned him in the first place

That's right. So, now how much is your husband worth?

30k?

No, don't you see, he's now only worth 15k. We've halved the value of a Kevin

I think I see. And that's a good thing, is it? No, sorry, I don't get it

Come on, we've known each other for forever and I'm pretty sure you'd still call yourself a feminist, wouldn't you?

You know I would. Of course I would

Well, isn't it obvious then? Halving the value of your husband is another step in undermining the patriarchy and bringing about greater gender equality. Which is what we all want isn't it?

Suppose so…

Isn't it?

No, I mean the first part, about undermining the patriarchy. How does loaning you Kevin do that?

Of course it does. But that's not the whole scheme. Here's the pure genius of it. Listen to this: While women up and down the country are loaning each other their husbands, at the same time we're taking out bets across a host of online platforms on the value of husbands

Hold on, rewind a bit. Women up and down the country?

Sure, this thing is going to be a coordinated effort, organised via social media. Thousands, maybe even millions of women are going to get involved. It's going to change everything

———

Right. And you're part of this what, this campaign?

That's right. You see, while these loans are taking place, simultaneously all these women are laying huge bets on the value of husbands going down

Okay, I think that makes sense, sort of

It surely does!

And, what, your idea is that Kevin come live with you, for a year?

No, don't be so silly! I don't mean to be rude, but why would I want that? I mean, Kevin. What we're talking about here is a nominal Kevin. Or a virtual Kevin, if you prefer

A virtual Kevin?

A nominal or virtual Kevin, it doesn't matter, and a virtual loan. Nothing actually needs to happen other than a bit of paperwork. Just a simple contract drawn up between us

Let me get this straight. You're proposing to pay me 15k to virtually loan my husband and then I pay you back the 15k at the end of the loan period? How long's the loan last?

As long or short as you like

And meanwhile we're betting shedloads on the value of husbands going down?

Millions, potentially

Which they surely must, if all these wives are doing the same thing?

You got it sister

That, that is sheer genius

Isn't it? It's the way the world goes round. So, what do you say? Do we have a deal?

Sure, why not

Great, I get that contract drawn up asap

Oh. Should I tell Kevin about this?

What do you think?

Right. I see

Right then, let's change the world. Let's make some serious money

———

The Op

To be honest, it was nice of them to bother to consult with the patients. Would she mind, they asked, if a new patient was moved into the ward in a bed close to hers? Of course she would not; why would she mind? She was very grateful for all the treatment she'd received and had no wish to be difficult. To tell them the truth, any new company would a breath of fresh air. After all, hadn't she had to put up with Mrs. Montgomery who was ninety and refused to be treated by coloured nurses or the pretty little, dark-haired nurse because she had tattooed arms. When that poor young nurse had tried to give the miserable old bat an injection one morning Mrs. Montgomery had shouted at the top of voice for her to go away because she unclean and disgusting.

Then there was Mrs. Chalmers s who hated needles and was suffering from dementia and kept offering to pay for the indifferent hospital food with a cheque book, as if she was lunching at a favourite restaurant. Mrs. Chalmers who could be heard all through the night lambasting her long dead husband for not dealing with their Sarah with a firm enough hand and also for dying, mortifyingly, with a penis that was altogether far too firm.

Of course, there was the nice little Indian woman opposite, a tiny wee thing who spoke hardly a word of English, with whom she'd managed to develop a friendship based on a shared rudimentary sign language of thumbs up and thumbs down. But really the nice Indian woman was the exception to the rule on the geriatric injury ward.

So when Leonard, the handsome young Cameroonian nurse, had

133

asked her about how she'd feel about a new ward companion and, as she was still rather whoozy after the op, she'd nodded her head without really thinking and said she was, why of course, she was perfectly happy. Why ever not?

So it had come as something of a shock when two large burly nurses had wheeled in a large cage, the sort of cage one might more usually have expected to see in a zoo. And more surprisingly still, when the cover was removed and inside those steel bars, there appeared to be some kind of full-grown big cat, probably from its spots, a leopard. And this leopard was prowling up and down and snarling, revealing its set of kitchen knife sized teeth.

Naturally she was rather concerned and expressed as much, indeed, had done so with considerable animation to Leonard. She spoke a little French and she did he. And so they'd fallen into the habit of exchanging some Gallic pleasantries each day. It had helped to divert both their attentions, especially when he had to carry out intimate examinations of her wounds. Vis-à-vis the leopard, she had, however, felt it more expedient to stick to the plainest and most direct forms of English phrasing.

Not only was having a large, possibly ravenous leopard on the ward highly disconcerting, in her opinion, and, she imagined, probably contrary to all health and safety regulations, the fact was that the door of its cage appeared to have carelessly been left open and she presumed, surely, this must have been some kind of a mistake. Frankly, she was sorry to have to tell him, but, in her opinion, it was highly irresponsible and, though she really hated to be a bother in the you know where, wasn't having a ferocious leopard on the ward, she wondered, liable to be something of a hostage to fortune? What, she asked Leonard as calmly as he could muster, would happen if the said

134

leopard got lose and started to predate on the largely prostate and entirely defenceless members of the ward? Even the fittest among them was painfully slow-moving. Surely in that life-and-death situation all these frail and elderly women wouldn't have a chance. She felt strongly that, in all probability, not one of them was likely to able to take down a full-grown leopard, not even Mrs. Montgomery, and even if they banded together and worked as a team to trap the beast, some of them would probably not live to tell the tale.

Nor did she expect Leonard or any of this colleagues to have to ride to the rescue. Of course, the NHS expected an awful lot from them, and they gave a lot and, it seemed, winningly did so too, to be sure. She had heard of catch-all contracts, but, nevertheless, surely she was right to presume that nothing in any of their contracts mentioned anything about tackling deadly big cats on the loose in a geriatrics ward. Common sense told her that the potential carnage that could ensure from having a leopard on a hospital ward was really best to be avoided.

'But, Mrs. James, can you not see the leopard is chained to the back of the cage,' the handsome Cameroonian nurse had said, with that broad, winning smile of his, 'really, I assure, you there is no need for you to worry. Really there is no danger.'

Well, even though he did have a lovely warm smile and a kind, gentle bedside manner and she'd admit only to herself, a rather trim, athletic backside, she still wasn't completely reassured.

'Why don't you just read your nice magazine and leave the other patients to our care?' Leonard added, patting her arm gently. He really did have such a lovely voice. So deep and calm and reassuring. He'd make someone a lovely husband, one day, she thought, suddenly

135

feeling an overpowering need to sleep.

Later, when her husband had come to visit her that evening with cards from the family and yet another bunch of blasted grapes, she'd immediately pointed out the cage to him and, to his great surprise and consternation, inside it, the increasingly snarly, presumably increasingly hungry leopard.

'Philip, would you be a dear and to do something about that leopard for me, there's a love. But do be careful, don't you get too close,' she said. 'Perhaps, if you'd be so kind, just try to shut the cage door for me. I'd be most grateful? Oh and Philip,' she said. 'No more grapes, there's a love. I don't even like them.'

Well, this really was considerably more than he'd bargained for when he'd decided to visit his wife in hospital. But, as ever, he didn't want to disappoint the love of his life. So, plucking up his courage, he moved slowly and steadily towards the cage. How stupid for the door to be left open and the beast to be left prowling up and down. But if he timed it just right and moved as quickly as his old bones would allow, he might just be able to push the cage door shut at the point when he was furthest away from the ravenous beast.

Unfortunately, the leopard was much faster than he'd thought. Or he was much slower. As soon as Philip had reached the door the beast had gone for him. Bounding with alarming velocity, it stretched its body and leapt like a wave into the air, claws extended, mouth pulled wide into a fearsome snarl. For a moment he feared those claws were about to rake down his chest and open his insides up like the proverbial tin of sardines. But somehow he managed to stagger backwards, hands raised in the air as if he'd been shot as the frustrated leopard reached the end of its chain and was yanked back into the cage.

———

136

If it weren't for the mortal danger, it would have been funny. In fact, Mrs. Montgomery did appear to be having a bit of chuckle. The mean old biddy.

As she munched on a grape, she watched her husband falling over backwards, as if in comical slow motion. She was both worried and amused at the same time. But then there was the most terrific crack. The sound of bone meeting concrete and then everything suddenly went black.

She was woken up, sweating, by a thump as something landed heavily near her bed. And then all she could hear was some plaintive meowing. Where on earth was that coming from? Looking down, she saw a small black and white, cat sitting staring with its big, cute eyes up at her in her hospital bed. It was Scraps, their long dead little cat. What on earth was she doing here? Scraps was meowing most pathetically. Probably she wanted to some milk or something tasty to eat. When she had a chance, she'd ask that nice young Canadian nurse, Bernard, to bring something for this strange cat.

Of her husband and the leopard there was absolutely no sign. And as the pale winter light fell through the hospital windows to lay supine across her bed, she knew for the first time that she certainly was going to get better.

Radio Ga-Ga

Mother was in the kitchen cooking dinner. Truth be told, his expectations weren't terribly high. Mother'd never been the most expert or enthusiastic of cooks and now she was getting on a bit. And her eyesight had been deteriorating steadily. On top of which, she wasn't used, these days, to cooking for guests. But despite his offer, she'd insisted she would cook. He didn't say anything, of course. Best not to hurt her feelings. And anyway there was the promise of some upside down pudding for afters.

Nevertheless it had come as a bit of a surprise when she'd informed them, with much apology, that she'd made a bit of a boo-boo with the portions and there might not be quite enough to go round. In fact, mother was going to have to serve her boys in two halves, the planned meal first - grilled gammon and veg. - and a quickly rustled-up substitute second.

Now the bar had been set even lower, they were pleasantly surprised when a full plate of steaming hot food was set down before oldest brother, Alec. A fragrant gammon steak, garnished with a pineapple ring, 1970's style, and a good heap of carrots and peas and plenty of delicious looking new potatoes, smeared with butter.

Alec was just about to tuck in with his usual relish when dad's dinner was placed before him. A similar looking plate, just with a slightly smaller pile of buttery spuds.

'Hold your horses, wait a moment,' he'd said as his brother had forked his first potato and was lifting it towards his eagerly gaping mouth, 'just wait to see if there's enough for mum and me.'

'Yes,' said father, nodding sagely, 'Alec, just wait until everyone's been served.'

Disappointedly, Alec put down his fork.

Next the plate of food prepared for him was delivered to the table.

'I'm sorry, love,' mother said as she placed it rather unsteadily before him, 'I'm afraid, it's all we had in.'

As his older brother and father tucked into their dinners, it was with considerable dismay that he surveyed his own meagre fare. Half a plate of last night's pasta, re-heated, with a sparse splattering of a pale-looking, watery cheese sauce.

Worse still, it seemed mother was not going to eat anything at all. She hadn't cooked enough food for everyone, she said. She would fill up later with cheese and biscuits after they'd eaten. It wasn't a problem. Honestly, she didn't have much of an appetite these days anyway. They were not to mind, she'd said. Go ahead, tuck in boys.

Of course, he wouldn't hear of it. Insisted on sharing half his pasta with her. Eventually, after much fuss, reluctantly, she acquiesced. And afterwards they'd shared a few stale crackers with some plastic cheese.

Later, on the phone, his wife had been outraged on his behalf. I hope you said something, she'd told him. That really just isn't fair. Poor love, you must be starving! You really shouldn't just put up with it. And you mustn't. It's because you've always put up with it and never complained. That's why it happens. Well you need to now. It's going way too far. This is ridiculous, love, absolutely ridiculous. Promise me you'll say something. Otherwise I will.'

Apologetically he explained that after they'd eaten, even though he found it awkward and difficult this time he had tried to speak to his parents, but to no avail.

I know it's difficult for Alec, he'd said, I'm fully aware of that. I have been all my life. And I totally understand that you feel you need to support and help him more... But there's an issue of fairness here...

He could sense, though, that mother was irked. The way she bristled and then cut him off abruptly.

'It's not so easy, for Alec, as you well know,' she said. 'Alec's always had it far harder than you and worse than ever since his illness.' She sounded really disappointed in him and he felt like he'd let her down and that he was behaving very selfishly. 'Remember you have had all the advantages in life,' she continued to scold him like a small boy, 'And you have far greater resources to draw upon than your brother, far greater. You got most of the brains, if not all of the looks. You went to University and have a great job, a successful wife, lovely kids... '

When finally mother had finished, he'd gone to the bathroom feeling a bit sick. There he was puzzled to find a radio sitting by the sink. Someone had left it on, and it was buzzing away quietly to itself. An old-fashioned radio. Obviously it hadn't been tuned in properly. A high female voice could be heard chattering away behind a wall of static, but he couldn't make out any words. The voice sounded familiar, but though he listened hard, he couldn't quite place it.

When he'd tried to tune it in, another voice suddenly sprang up at him out of the ether. This second voice was very loud and crystal clear. Male, deep and resonant, it could have been the voice of Morgan Freeman or, perhaps, the voice of God.

'Why don't you stop being all high and mighty?' the deep voice admonished him, 'sitting self-righteously on your moral high horse. Poor little you. If you're so goddamn concerned with equity, why isn't your little sis in this dream? Doesn't she deserve even to be at the table when dinner is finally served?'

At which point, guiltily, Justin awoke.

The Shot

When, finally, he'd got there, after the long, difficult ride through the middle of the night, he hadn't really a clue what to do with him. He was only an inexperienced auxiliary policeman, after all, and had not been given the job because he was particularly keen to do it or because he had demonstrated any great aptitude for policing. Or, in truth, had to demonstrate anything much at all. No, he'd got the job solely because he owned his own motorbike. And what training he'd had, well that had been pretty rudimentary, even for these days.

And now he could see the farm outbuildings looming up in the bike's front light, he remembered, with not a little trepidation, that he wasn't carrying a truncheon, let alone a pistol.

He had had the devil's own time even finding this farm. Stopping frequently to check his bearings on his map by the light of his torch, he had, in fact, taken a few wrong turns and had to double back on himself several times. The farm really was out in the sticks, literally in the middle of nowhere, over the border and into wild and rugged rural Wales. Fortunately for him, the spring weather was fine and the farm wasn't too far off a half-decent A-road. Though the last leg of trip, in the early morning dimness, down a long, bumpy, winding track had been a challenge on the bike, even for him.

According to sarge, a Welsh farming couple had captured the German. A plane had crashed in fields near their farm and the man he'd been sent to arrest had been the only survivor. The farmers had heard the plane going over, then the crash and bravely set off into the fading evening light to investigate. With their torches and their trusty sheep dog, carrying only farm implements for protection, they'd located the wreck, then found the only survivor, trapped inside the ruined plane, and had managed to pull him clear of the wreckage. Though he might not thank them for it, in doing so they had certainly saved his life.

Apparently, the German airman was a bit dazed and his uniform was badly burnt around the edges, but, it seemed otherwise he was largely uninjured. Once they'd frog marched him by torchlight back to their farm, the husband had stood guard, while his wife phoned the police for help.

And so here was, the help.

The farmer's wife waved at him as he pulled the bike, gratefully, into the yard. She was a large, ruddy, excitable woman, dressed, he noticed, in a big, heavy coat, pulled tight with a belt - probably this had been flung hastily over nightclothes. As he slipped and slid a little in the soggy mud of the yard, he wished that, like her, he too was wearing a pair of stout wellies.

Taking him firmly by the arm, chatting volubly, the woman was evidently very keen for him to come and see the great work they had done in capturing one of the enemy.

'We've got him!' she told him, gesticulating towards one of the large barns, 'In the barn. My hubby's doing the guarding. He's not getting away from us, that bloody Kraut, not over my dead body.'

Moments later, the farmer's wife was opening the barn door and excitedly ushering him into the semi-darkness within.

In the gloomy half-light of the barn, he could just about make out two figures in one corner. A squat, stocky figure pointing some sort of long instrument at another smaller figure, seemingly backed up against a wall.

'Hello,' he called nervously into the large echoing space. As he walked cautiously towards them his eyes adjusted slowly to the dimness, 'I'm the police, sent over to help.'

'Over here,' the farmer called over his shoulder. 'Here, in the corner. Don't worry, I've got the bugger surrounded. He's not going nowhere.'

Once he drew close enough, he could see that the captured German was only a young man, perhaps only eighteen years old or so. Cornering him against the barn wall was a hefty, rugged-looking Welsh farmer, braced and pointing what he now realised was an alarmingly large pitchfork, straight at the young German's neck. Sharp, curved prongs hovered only inches away from the pale, exposed flesh and the young man was shaking uncontrollably, probably with a combination of shock and fear.

The airman was a Kraut, of course, one of the hated enemy. A Kraut airman whose plane had come down, killing the rest of the crew. Must have been a bomber, he thought, a bomber that would, otherwise, have shed its load of death over Liverpool or perhaps Manchester or even closer to home. But this young, pathetic-looking wretch in the half-light of the barn was also just a frightened young man. Not even that, really. More like a boy. In his ragged, half-singed uniform, cowering back against the wall, he cut a pitiable figure. He was no match at all for the large, ruddy Welsh farmer wielding the pitchfork.

Although he was policeman, albeit only an auxiliary one, and as such, a guardian of the British realm, and although his beloved, older brother, Walt, had been killed by Germans during the Great War, he felt no great enmity towards Germany or the German people per se. Nor did he feel any enmity towards this poor, traumatized boy. And truth be told, in peacetime, as a proud Englishman who lived and worked just the other side of the border, he tended to harbour less than generous feelings towards the Welsh.

They could be sly, the Welsh, in his experience, and, in the business dealings he had with them, sometimes untrustworthy. Bit a chip on their shoulders, some of them, a bit hostile to the English. And more than a few times he'd had to deal with young Welsh farmers who'd come into town on a weekend and had a skinful and got a bit too rowdy. Once, one of them had given him a nasty black eye for his troubles. No, he wasn't a big fan of the Welsh, in all honesty. But this probably wasn't the right time to reveal such ambivalent feelings.

'What you going to do with him, boyo?'

That, indeed, was the question. What was he supposed to do with him?

Gratefully he remembered then that his youngest daughter had taught him how to speak a few words of German, because, she thought, they might just come in handy one day. If the Germans invaded, for instance, she'd said blithely. Clever little Jane. It was worth giving the German lingo a go, even if he'd feel a bit of a fool, especially in front of someone else, doing the funny accent and whatnot.

'Heine Hinde,' he said as he walked right up to the German, 'heine hinde'.

But, he must have got the words wrong, because the young man just

---

stared at him blankly and didn't put his hands up in the air, as he had been instructed. Perhaps the German lad was still a bit dazed. If he just raised his voice a little it might make the words easier for him to understand. 'HEINE HINDE,' he shouted, 'HEINE HINDE'.

Strangely, there was still no response, except for a look of puzzlement on the young man's pale and sickly-looking face.

Perhaps he should give another one of his phrases a go. 'Sprechen die Deutsch?' he asked, pointing to his mouth, he hoped, expressively, 'Sprechen die Deutsch?'

'Ja,' the young man replied hesitantly, taken aback, he expected, by hearing someone speaking in his own language in this god-forsaken backwater. This was a good sign, surely. Now they were beginning to make progress. He clapped his hands together, smiled at the farmer and nodded to indicate that he and the German were now firmly on the same wavelength. If the farmer was impressed, he showed no sign of it. Clearly he had no intention of dropping his guard with the pitchfork.

'Right then,' he coughed and tried to sound like he knew what the hell he was doing, 'put your hands up and keep them there, ja? Comprendo?' He'd better frisk the German, just to make sure he hadn't a weapon hidden somewhere on his person.

Next he had to decide how to get his young prisoner back to the nick. The farmer didn't have a car, so they'd have to go on the back of the motorbike. That much was clear already. But what would prevent the captive from trying to escape or forcing him to crash the bike at some opportune moment? There was only one thing for it. They'd have to tie the German up and then lash the two of them together on the bike.

All it would need was some good, strong rope. Not difficult to find on a farm, he expected.

✳

It was a long, tiring and difficult journey back through the morning traffic. They must have looked an odd pair to any of their few fellow early morning travelers. Him in his auxiliary uniform, the German in his singed airman's clothes, bound together with thick rope, bent over the bike's handlebars. Whatever they looked like, having a rigid weight on his back made riding far more of a challenge, especially around tight corners. He was conscientious too of their awkward physical proximity. The smell of the burnt clothes and the young man's rancid sweat, the constant pressure of the German's chest on his back, the ragged sounds of his breathing. Even, sometimes, with a shiver, the touch of his cold breath on his exposed neck.

By the time they reached the house, he was desperate for a cup of hot, sweet tea and something tasty to eat. It'd been a long, long night and he was almost dead on his feet. He'd stop off at home for a while to get some refreshments and then hop back on the bike and run the German the last leg of the journey to the city jail. Thinking about it, he realized, his prisoner might also need something to keep him going.

As he untied the rope that had bound them so closely together and the two men stood, gratefully apart and stared at each other, a new problem became apparent.

The young German was urgently trying to tell him something. He could just about pick out a few of the unfamiliar sounding words 'Urineren', 'Ick' something or other he didn't catch. And then, again, 'urineren'. It took a few more moments and some frantic gesturing and hopping from one foot to the other by the German before he realised the young man desperately needed a piss. There was nothing for it - he'd have to untie him, at least partially. Instinct told him that this pathetic-looking, traumatised young man wasn't dangerous. But he still needed to be careful. It could be some sort of ruse. Would his captive try to make a run for it, or, his hands loose, even attack him somehow perhaps? No, looking at the pitiful figure, he really didn't think that was possible.

When Nessie came to the door and saw her husband standing framed there, looking a tired and a little sheepish in the bright spring sunlight, with some sort of prisoner half-a-pace behind him, a prisoner who was still, she quickly noticed, at least partially tied up with a rope, she'd immediately made it quite clear, in the most forthright of terms possible that, no, there was no way on this earth that she was going to allow a dangerous prisoner, let alone this one, who, unless she was very much mistaken, from the charred uniform appeared to be some kind of a German, i.e. one the mortal enemy. Did she need to remind her husband, Germans were from Germany, Germany with whom they were currently at war. No way was a German going to come into her own house, let alone use their posh new lavatory. Was he completely out his mind? Not on his nelly.

Nor, did it seem, though she was, no doubt, relieved to see her husband safely back from his night-time excursion, keen to provide tea and cake for anyone. And especially not for his captive. But, once she'd cooled down a bit, she'd taken pity on them both and would bring out two mugs of hot tea and some sandwiches, to be consumed, mind you, strictly within the confines of the garden and nowhere else.

So, there was nothing for it. He'd have to take his prisoner down to the bottom of the garden where he would be able to relieve himself in the bushes. He was going to have to loosen the hands a little to allow

---

148

this, of course. The garden was surrounded by a wooden fence, so even if the German did make a run for it, he wouldn't be able to get very far. And there was no way he could have any weapon on him - he'd frisked him himself thoroughly a couple of times to make double sure.

So it was he found himself standing at the bottom of his own garden, standing discretely, just a little way back, yawning, enjoying the warmth of the spring sun on his tired skin. All around him birds singing in the shrubs and up in the trees, accompanied by the sound of a young German airman pissing into the bushes.

And that was the last thing he heard.

Pull yourself together Jacko

Really she couldn't understand what all the fuss was about, all the tears, all the crying. Of course it was sad that he had died, it was very sad, she wasn't saying it wasn't. Of course not. But, as she had told her teary younger sister when she'd come to visit a few days after the funeral, in many ways, frankly, it was also a relief, a relief for all of them. At least now her son was at peace and the ravages of the last few years were finally over.

She'd told her sister how she'd noticed her granddaughter snivelling and sniffling all the way through the service and afterwards too. She didn't approve, of course, and had said so, in no uncertain terms and was saying so again now. Wasn't that her prerogative as the mother? Why should she have to apologise? There was no need for such a display of, well, weakness. The girl wasn't a child; she was a young adult and ought to behave like an adult. What she needed was to toughen up a bit that girl. Otherwise how would she ever cope with everything life can throw at you?

Hadn't she herself had to toughen up pretty darn quickly all those years ago, when mother's body had finally been fished out of the canal? She still remembered like it was yesterday. The policeman informing father of the death and him crying like a baby; the first time she had ever seen him crying. Of course, she too had cried then, cried an awful lot, in fact. She wasn't ashamed to admit it. But she'd only been a young woman, not much more than a girl, then and had had the most terrible shock imaginable. As far as she could recall, she hadn't ever cried since, not once in over half a century. Not even at her mother's funeral.

She'd toughened up, that was why. She'd had to. What choice did she have? What did crying ever achieve anyway? Absolutely nothing, that's what. Would crying have propped up dad or supported her little brother and sister? Would moping around feeling sorry for herself kept the house and the family together through thick and thin during the toughest of times? Did crying help you to pick up the pieces when your life was shattered into thousands of parts? No, she didn't think so. She wasn't the sort of woman who cried at the drop of the hat and there was no way she was about to start emoting all over the place now, especially not in front of other people. You had to be strong and stoical, not just for yourself, but everyone else, for the rest of the family.

A few years back, the same younger sister who was perched now on the sofa opposite had warned her that her son was fighting a losing battle against the demon drink.

'Rubbish,' she'd snapped, 'Absolute rubbish.' Hadn't she worked with him every day at the Post Office? If he'd have been an alcoholic, did they really think she wouldn't have noticed? Of course she would. Did they think she was an idiot?

Yes, okay, Tony liked a drink or two, she'd never denied that. For that record, nor had he. So what? Who doesn't like a drink or two from time to time? She certainly did, as did Jacko. Her younger sister's husband's another one - he certainly liked a drink. He never said no to a top-up and nobody batted an eye about that, did they, or made accusations about alcoholism. Remember that time on holiday when they'd drunk a bottle of whisky between the three of them in just one evening?

The temerity, the effrontery of her sister's accusation had felt like a slap across her face. It stung. She'd dismissed the crazy idea out-of-hand at the time, of course. What else could she do but swat it aside without a second thought? It was intolerable, it was insufferable having anyone, let alone her much younger sister sitting in her house blithely telling her that her son was a pathetic, hopeless, pitiful drunk. No, not our Tony. No, no way. It wasn't true. It just couldn't be true. She would not allow it to be true.

'He's not an alcoholic. You'll see. He's strong, strong as stone, like me,' she had said, fixing her sister in the glare she'd used frequently when they were children, daring her to disagree.

Of course she knew she wasn't absolutely infallible, though not too far off it most of the time. Some people were just more right about things and more often right than others. Some people might have gone off to university, but others had had to learn life the hard way, in the school of hard knocks. And on this matter, her sister was wrong and she was right.

Jacko had said nothing, just kept his own counsel, as usual, and offered to top up everyone's drinks. Probably he didn't want to be drawn into a family row. Her husband was a lovely man, kind and gentle. A good man. But in her heart she knew he was not as strong as her. Perhaps that was where her son had inherited it from, that lack of robustness.

Because it transpired that her sister was right. That her son, in fact, had been weak, fatally weak. But his problems had only started to escalate once the Post Office had installed that blasted new computer system. Each week thereafter the takings were short and soon he was having to top them up from his life savings, or face being accused of theft by his employers. Soon, to his bitter humiliation, he'd had go cap in hand to his elderly parents to borrow more money to make up the weekly shortfalls. Thousands and thousands of pounds in the end. How was he to know that he wasn't the only sub-postmaster struggling with this issue? As far as he ever knew from his employers, the new computer system was working perfectly and he was the only sub-postmaster who was having these problems. So the shortfalls were all down to him.

Over the months and years, the strain became too great, on him, on his family, on his marriage and it was then that he had increasingly sought an escape from it all in drink.

Yes, it was sad, it was very sad. His marriage to the lovely wife, of whom she'd always approved, had started to crumble. She had started to talk about wanting a divorce. Who could blame her for that? She didn't, certainly. And Tony's drinking just got heavier and more frequent until it spun completely out of control.

Eventually he'd drunk a bottle of whisky sitting in his car, then stepped out in front of a bus rushing down an A-road. The poor driver – she felt terribly sorry for him. There was nothing he could have done. Tony hadn't been killed instantly. For a few long weeks they'd kept him unconscious and barely alive on a machine in the hospital. She'd visited him, visited him every day, held his hand, brushed his beautiful blond hair from his face and talked to him, all the time, although the doctors weren't sure he could hear her, or could hear anything else, for that matter. A vegetative state, that's what they called it. If he'd survived, he would, they told her, have been a vegetable for life. Well, what sort of life would that be?

When after nearly a month there'd still been no signs of improvement and the chances of recovery were almost zero, the decision had been made to pull the plug on the life support machine and let him die finally in peace.

No, she hadn't cried then. Nor had she cried during his recent funeral, nor would she just a few years later, when Jacko died. And certainly not now either, she wasn't going to cry, talking about it all to her younger sister and her husband who had kindly come to stay with them for a few days.

'It's sad, very sad,' she said, draining her drink, 'but at least now he's at peace.'

And now when her younger sister had got up to embrace Jacko, well, at that point for some reason the dams had really burst. His face had just melted and he was suddenly in floods of tears, his body shaking, like a child again.

She couldn't help it, but a huge surge of fury coursed through her body. Like a great wave, rolling through her, coursing through her veins, building and building. She felt utterly alight with fury. At that moment, she might easily have got up and knocked her husband to the ground.

'Pull yourself together Jacko,' she had shouted at him, shouted with all the stored-up hardness of her soul, 'just pull yourself together.'

And then, when he looked back at her in that shocked and desperate way, the tears streaming from his tired old eyes, the great wave crashed in her heart, and she suddenly knew that in her whole life, she'd never loved him so much.

What a Drag!

It was the costumes that really dazzled. And the transformation, the massive, massive transformation. One minute there was a guy, some ordinary guy a bit like me – an awkward guy, gawky, a bit shy, a social misfit perhaps and then the next minute he was this totally amazing, diva, sashaying about in high-heeled boots, black fishnets, skirt up to the arse. Big loopy earrings, ruby red lipstick and the most gorgeous long black wig - glorious black curls, falling like waves all the way down to the waist. Sparkly satiny top, and tits, I mean, massive, massive tits. Well. Blew me clean away. I mean. I mean, wow. There's power in that, I thought to myself. Real power, like electricity. Why shouldn't I have a bit of that? Why not, thank you very much, I thought. I will, I thought. You just stand back and watch me, I thought.

Totally surprised myself. Didn't know I had this, any of this, inside of me. Up until that moment I'd thought men dressed as women were comical – pantomime dames, Lily Savage, that sort of thing. Or transvestites. But, in that moment under those dazzling lights, something was released in me, an energy, a vitality, and everything just, it just completely changed.

We all of us have many other selves, don't you think? Other characters inside us. Shadow selves? And mostly, for most of us, most of the time, that's where they remain, in the darkness. Of course we do. And this thing, opened a window, a window through which my wildest, craziest, most fabulous shadow self could fly into the light, like a bird. To really let everything just rip, for once. Absolutely no brakes. Absolutely no holds barred. How exhilarating is that? Especially for someone like me,

155

who since I was, I don't know, ten years old had had to hold everything in, keep it all pressed down, crabbed and contained. But up on that stage, in the dazzling lights, I would be able to be anything, do anything, be free. No constraint, no restraint, but, boy oh boy, plenty of paint. That, I thought, would be my motto. That's how it all started.

I soon learnt that in order to progress you have to get a good Drag Mother – that's the key to any proper, long-term career. Someone fiercer than you, someone braver, someone tougher. Someone who's got a few miles on the clock, been about a bit, if you know what I mean. Smart and savvy. Worthy of respect. They take you under their wing, a bit like a mother hen. Show you the ropes, while you're still a bit green in the gills. Yes, is it like an apprenticeship scheme or a protégé style thing.

Well, for me that person was the utterly marvellous Miss Melody Sumptuous. What an awesome, awesome lady! She was my big break, my stroke of unbelievable good fortune or destiny maybe, coming across her or, rather, the other way round. She'd seen my act, such as it was, when I first gave it a go and, somehow'd seen some potential, though at first, on stage, I was nervous as hell. Soon she was giving me all the essential tips – the right foundation for my skin tone, the cutest lipstick, the wildest costumes, where to buy them, the best songs for my type of voice. Everything I needed really. Otherwise, I'd have been lost.

Normally, before, at parties, with mates or the family, as myself, though I always knew I'd a voice, a good voice, unless I'd had a skinful, I'd be far too self-conscious to get up and sing. The wife, she could always make me feel almost ashamed of myself, especially after she'd had a few too many herself. But in my full get-up, head to foot in utter glittering, sparkling gorgeousness, strutting my stuff on stage at the

Pink Valhalla, well I could finally let everything just go. I didn't need alcohol - I'd belt out those tunes, bold and brassy as hell, and it felt like I was lifted up and carried along on a great wave.

The make-up and the clothes, they're armour aren't they? You put it on and you feel like a completely different person. You are a different person - stronger, braver, tougher. Sexier too. My God, so much sexier! Goodbye boring old, awkward old Kev and say hello to the fabulous Miss Precious Mandalay. That was the name I chose, after a while, once it had all got more serious. You have to build a name and a whole new identity for yourself, a kind of alter ego, if you like, a brand. Think differently, speak differently, move differently. Give your shadow substance. Soon that was who I felt I really was, my true, real, inner self, Precious. On stage, as her was when, you know, I was most truly alive and most fully me.

Didn't I worry that the wife would find out? Of course, naturally, who wouldn't? We've been married for years. I loved her, in my own limited way. Melody understood. She'd seen it all before. So, at first, we kept all my outfits at her place. That's where I'd get changed ready for the club. Metamorphosise is more like. Growing and spreading my fabulous fairy wings. Melody said it was incredible, that in a long career, she'd never seen such a miraculous transformation. Dull caterpillar to fabulous butterfly. I'll take that, I thought, I'll take that.

At first I only went to the club once in a while and it was easy enough to lie about what I got up to. The wife wasn't must interested in what I did in my own time, not those days. The club was quite a way away from the town where we live, so nobody knew me there. Not that they were likely to recognise me, not in my full regalia.

Sometimes I wanted to laugh in her face, the wife's and then tell her everything. Confess. Not because I felt guilty, because I totally didn't. But, you know, just to see her jaw drop and eyes pop out – to see the look of utter stupefaction on her face. She'd never have imagined it. Not in a million years. Her Kevin, a drag queen? Don't be so bloody ridiculous. Get off, pull the other one. Dull, dependable, steady old Kevin? Don't be so bloody daft.

Honestly, it was like being a drug addict. Totally compelling, total intoxication. Soon I was craving more, as much as I could possibly get. Got careless, I suppose. Keeping these two selves so separate, that was hard too, too hard. Sometimes when I was being Kev, at work say or down the pub with my mates, a little bit of Precious would slip out, a word or a phrase, a gesture maybe. And people would give me an old look or ask me if I was feeling alright.

Even as good old, dull old Kev, I was a different man now. It's hard to explain, but, I'd always lacked confidence. I was awkward around other people. Shy, I suppose. Probably something to do with my childhood. I don't think I ever really liked myself. But Precious, boy, she absolutely loved herself, oh my God, big time. And that kind of filled me with light, with air, with great pulsing waves of joy like I'd felt before, coursing through me, lifting me up, carrying me and I think that light, it shone out of old Kev's eyes too, at times. I just couldn't keep all that effervescence bottled up.

And then one night, I saw him. Out there in the audience, dancing under a flashing white strobe. He was near the front, watching me all the time on the stage. His look was so close, so intimate, so tender. Honestly, it was like being touched. He didn't take his eyes off me, not for a single moment, during the whole set.

Young, black, very good looking. Lean, athletic body. Nice, shy smile.

Jesus, it was like Romeo and bloody Juliet, only, well, you know, two blokes. One of whom was dressed in drag. Crazy, I know.

And after my turn, there's a knock on my changing room door. My heart's pounding like a bloody drum. Fortunately, I'm still all glammed up - I change at Melody's - and I was just having a breather and a ciggie after the show. Now, this is going to sound really strange. Probably you're not going to believe me, but I've never been attracted to a man before, not really, not like that, not in that way.

Sexually, I mean. I'm not, or I wasn't, ever, you know, before. Or if I was, I sure didn't know. For me, this whole thing was just a dressing up thing, like acting, only bolder and bigger. I never actually wanted to be a woman.

The next few months, whenever I was on stage, singing my once timid little heart out, there he'd be on the dance floor, watching and listening and smiling and nodding. That first time, he'd told me he was totally bowled over, infatuated. That he'd never felt like this before about anyone. I was a goddess. I had enchanted him. That I had put him under my spell and he was my slave, he said. He would do anything for me, he said. He said that he loved me. He loved. Me.

I daren't take it any further. Didn't really know whether I wanted to or not. Whether I could. I was curious, I'm not ashamed to admit that, but also hesitant, wary. I did find him attractive, yes, very attractive. There was something feminine and almost feline about him, which helped. But, you know, I'd never… And then, one evening, I got to wondering whether it was just Precious that he was really infatuated with and not, you know, the rest of me.

First chance I had, I made my excuses, said I had a nasty head cold and couldn't sing and went to the Pink Valhalla just dressed as my old self. Not as Precious, but as good old, dull old Kev.

Of course, I dressed up a bit for the club. Put on a bit of costume. Otherwise I'd have stood out like a sore thumb in my usual jeans and polo. I'd confided in Melody, who else, and she'd found some appropriate gear to wear.

God, I was nervous. Like a teenager with a first crush. Without my full regalia, without my make-up and wig, without my armour, I felt naked, exposed. But I was determined too. I still had that light buoying me up from the inside. So I pushed my way to the bar, downed a quick martini or two and then started to look around the place.

Another act was on stage, my last-minute replacement. Fabulous costume, all in red, not much a of voice. You don't go far in the drag business if you haven't really got a voice, even if you look the part. Anyway, I couldn't see him on the dancefloor and for a moment I was afraid he hadn't come.

But then there he was. Towards the back of the room, nursing a drink, on his own. So handsome. I took the deepest of breaths, necked my drink and headed over.

He looked up.

'Hello,' I said, hoping he'd recognise the voice.

'Alright.'

I looked in his eyes for any signs of recognition.

'Look. What do you want, mate?' he said, taking a swig from his bottle of lager.

I didn't know what to say.

'Listen, mate. Do I know you?'

I wanted to shout, it's me, can't you see, it's me, Precious, just without all the crazy glitzy get-up. It's me, Kevin.

It's still me. It's really me.

'Look mate, no offence or anything,' he looked over my shoulder, as if looking for an excuse to move away. 'I'm really not interested. Okay?'

Okay.

'Sorry, mate.'

And with that he turned and just walked away.

One for Sorrow

Bloody magpies. It made no sense, it made no sense at all. How could it possibly work? For entirely obscure and mysterious reasons, some sort of consciousness that governs the workings of the universe, already a thought step he wasn't prepared to take, but anyway, putting that to one side for a moment, this consciousness had decided, with motives entirely unknown, that it was necessary to communicate, from time to time, a human being's predetermined allocation of good and bad luck over an indeterminate duration to him, or her, and that the ideal delivery method for such intimations was through the appearance, or not, of a rattling black and white bird, or birds, of, he believed, the crow family, birds which turn up frequently in parks and gardens and steal other birds' eggs. Not through robins, or sparrows, or pigeons, or goldfinches, say. Or none-bird-related communication channels. But, uniquely, this important, potentially life-shaping information had to be communicated exclusively through magpies. Which rather begged the question, why magpies? And for that matter, why birds? What sort of crazy, half-baked language was that? And, more to the point, what sort of crazy, half-baked speaker?

Of course, more superstitious and more spiritual minded folk find the promise good or the threat bad fortune in all sorts of mysterious signs and miracles. A black cat crossing your path, seeing a comet, reading your fate in the stars etc. etc. and so and so forth. But, perhaps, he hadn't been exposed to those particular fears at an impressionable enough age for they exerted on grip on his imagination. Furthermore, he'd had a black cat as a kid and, granted, he might not have studied the phenomena systematically, but he was pretty sure there was no clear correlation between appearances of Huckleberry and good or bad luck befalling him or any of his family.

But magpies. They were another matter entirely.

He'd seen one that morning, out of the bedroom window as he was getting changed after his shower. He'd just happened to be looking at the garden at the precise moment the bird had flown rather clumsily up into a tree and then set off in its distinctively stuttering flight across the pale blue sky. And at that very moment, that precise moment, he'd been thinking of his mother. And now, as he towelled himself dry, try as he might, he couldn't shake off a feeling of dread. It was stupid. He knew that. But he felt it anyway. A definite sense of dread.

Normally he prided himself on being decidedly and completely rational. He didn't believe in God, or gods, nor any of that sort of superstitious moonshine. Never had done so as far as he could recall. He couldn't remember believing in any form of deity even as a young child. He wasn't one of those people who grow up and shrug off religious faith alongside belief in Father Christmas, fairies and magic wishes. His parents hadn't been religious, so it just hadn't ever been part of his life. If he had have believed in a deity, he'd have been tempted, perhaps, to pray to him/her/it/them now. But he didn't and so he didn't.

But magpies.

He was staying for the weekend at his elderly parents' house, looking after his dad and waiting for more news. Mum was still in hospital, recovering, they hoped fervently, from a nasty fall in the bathroom that had fractured her hip. The accident would have been bad enough at any time, but during a pandemic? The timing couldn't have been any worse.

And it wasn't just mum he was worried about; dad was also concerning him. When he answered the door yesterday, his face had been ashen, drained by tiredness and worry, and all evening he distractedly stroked his new grey beard, as if desperately seeking reassurance in it. Worse, he kept forgetting what he was doing. Walking into a room and then standing vaguely about, looking at a bit of a loss. That just wasn't like dad. His mind had always been sharp as a tack. How was this newly anxious, uncertain, shuffling version of dad going to manage when mum was finally released from hospital, entirely dependent on him for help and support and cooking?

Of course, some people claimed to be able to read the future in tea leaves or through gazing into a crystal ball or palm reading. Or they read about it in the pages of a cheap tabloid. One, he didn't believe in fate. That was not how the universe operated. Two, all claims to clairvoyancy were obviously specious claptrap, exploiting the credulous and needy. Astronomy, like religion, but even worse, was complete and utter hogwash. Superstitions were for children, the ignorant and the feeble minded. He'd no time either for any foolish talk of curses, evil spirits or lucky charms. It staggered him that even some relatively rational people he knew, people who held down good jobs and generally didn't talk lie gibbering lunatics believed in ghosts. Loose spirits? Loose brains, more like. Frankly, he found such beliefs laughable and, in certain moods, wasn't afraid to say so.

But magpies. Why did they still bother him so? It made zero sense.

When, after breakfast, he had gone for a walk round the local park, they were everywhere. He'd had to get out for a bit to clear his head and escape into the fresh air. And at almost every turn of the path, he'd hear the rattle of the blasted black and white birds. Which had brought to mind another tricky point of magpie lore. What did it mean if you saw one magpie on its own and then, moments later, another one, also on its own? Did the second sighting double the bad luck? Or, because now you'd seen two in total did the second one switch the bad luck coming your way into good luck? Or might magical magpie power not work like that? Perhaps, it was, in fact, a coded sequence; the first single bird signalled bad luck would befall you and then the second, making two magpies, signalled that good luck would follow?

If that were the case, he could expect, from this morning's encounters, a sequence of good, bad, bad, good, bad, girl, bad, good, bad, boy, bad. Or something like that – in truth he'd lost count. And what exactly was the time span over which this process operated? Were these incidents of good and bad fortune going to occur at evenly spaced intervals, perhaps one per day? Or would the pattern be much more irregular and cover a much longer, or indeed shorter, period of time? If the former, what happened if he saw more magpies in the meantime? Did later magpies cancel out the malign or benign influence of earlier ones or amplify their positive or negative effect? Really it was a puzzle. The sort of muddle that gave even the ablest philosophers headaches.

Mum had been in hospital for well over a week now. They'd hoped to get her out sooner, after the op., but apparently her salts had been low. Dad suspected that the social services hadn't managed to put the 'care package' in place yet and they were stalling for time. For his part, he imagined the hospital staff must be utterly exhausted and just struggling to keep things ticking over as best they could. He was sure they were doing their utmost and he trusted implicitly in their medical expertise. Superstition was hokum, but science was something in which he had complete faith. Well, most of the time.

Mulling over the various magpie dilemmas, he circled the bluey grey water of the lake. Noisy geese, ducks, moorhens and the spring light sparkling on the water. Imagine if that non-existent, perverse and mysterious consciousness had chosen one of those birds, instead, he thought. Why not? In that case, a completely different scale would be required, there were so many of them. Perhaps a decimal scale would work: Ten ducks = bad luck; twenty = good luck and so on.

Yes, but then that thew up the problem of different types of duck. Would a mallard count the same as wigeon or a shoveler? And that in turn introduced another knotty technical difficulty. What about people who were unable to tell one type of duck from another or, indeed, a duck from a goose or moorhen? How would these people receive accurate intimations of future fortune, good or bad, through ducks? It'd just never work. Only a complete imbecile would put on a bet, say, thinking he had good luck coming, on such shaky grounds. He had to admit, in that sense, using easily identifiable birds, such as magpies did seem the better, more logical option, when one really thought about it.

In the still spindly trees surrounding the lake, patches of blossom were just starting to come out, pale pinks and delicate, frilly whites. He could hear various other non-luck related birds singing. Robins and blackbirds mostly. That two-note call could, he thought, be a great tit. Or perhaps a chiff-chaff. Really he was no expert. What if you heard a magpie, but didn't see it, but knew it was there? Did that count or not?

Mum hadn't been allowed to speak much on the phone and, of course, during the pandemic visiting the hospital was prohibited. From their brief snippets of conversation and the text messages and through what he'd gleaned from dad, the nurses had apparently been 'angels', but staying on the ward had been 'pretty grim'. Distressed and confused old people on her ward. One a dementia patient, calling out all night. Mum probably wasn't telling them the worst, putting a brave face on things, no doubt. As usual, being stoical. But, certainly, the sooner she was out of there, the better.

The weather had been unseasonably warm for a while now and he found that, even in just his shirtsleeves and without a jacket, that he was soon perspiring lightly. He had been striding out rather. It helped to burn calories and keep the weight off. And the exertion helped to clear his mind. Were magpies cursed because of something to do with weeping or not weeping at Christ's crucifixion? He'd read that somewhere. Was that why they were considered bad luck?

The mistake many people made, of course, was to confuse sequential relationships with consequential ones. As in, mistaking X happened after y happened for x happened because y happened. It was a common error and humans were particularly prone to it, seeing everywhere significances in mere coincidence. Correlation is not causation, he remembered his grandfather used to say. Even his otherwise rational sister would say how spooky it was that she sometimes sensed when mum was going to phone her, before she actually rang. Yeah, right, spooky, except that mum nearly always rang him at the same time each week, and probably her too.

By the time he was leaving the park and setting off for home, he reckoned he must have seen about twenty magpies. Mostly on their own, but also quite a few in pairs. So, what did that portend? What was it again you were supposed to do on seeing one magpie? Salute it, stand on one leg, close an eye and saying something like, 'Good afternoon, Mr. Magpie'. Was that it? Or was it maybe 'Hello, Jack, how's your father?' And then, did you spit on the floor? Well, whatever bad luck might accrue, he'd have to take it. He'd never done any of

---

167

that and he certainly wasn't going to start doing so now, especially not in front of other people. Anyhow, he knew there was absolutely nothing in it. Just a stupid, stupid, childish superstition. But one he still couldn't quite rid himself of. It was like chewing gum, just kept sticking to him. And then there'd been so many of the birds, uncannily crossing his path today. It was strange. He'd never seen so many. Hence this nagging sense of unease.

It looked like it was going to turn out to be a nice day. Not many clouds in the blue sky. The air fresh and crisp. A soft, gentle breeze. Warming up very nicely. No dark clouds to presage disaster. But, then again, dad was in charge of lunch, so who knew what they'd be eating.

Stupid, of course. Ridiculous. Utterly absurd. He must push it from his mind. He wasn't a cretin. Or a child. But how would he feel if bad luck came on him now or, worse on his mother because pride had stopped him going through with the approved ritual for warding off bad magpie luck? Could he get home and then make up for this by performing the rituals alone in the guest bedroom? He'd have to look them up to make sure he got them right. Or did the manoeuvres and accompanying invocations have to be completed immediately on seeing the single magpie? These were the sorts of tricky questions of doctrine that had kept theologians in business down the centuries.

He saw his last, single magpie as he had crossed the road out of the park. The driver said he'd just stepped off the pavement, not looking, distracted, as if his mind was entirely elsewhere. Weirdly, she thought, he'd raised one hand to his face, in a gesture that looked a bit like a salute.

She'd immediately slammed on her brakes, as hard as she could. Had tried desperately to swerve out of the way. But the wheels must have

---

hit a piece of ice on the road. Because the car just skidded, out of control and the impact was unavoidable.

There was nothing she could have done. She just really hadn't been expecting ice on the roads, not in Spring. Not on such a bright, warm and sunny day.

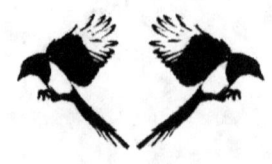

About the Author

Neil Bowen is an English teacher, presenter and author. He is the co-author of a range of critical guide on literary texts in 'The Art of Poetry', 'The Art of Drama' and 'The Art of Literature' series. This is his debut collection of short stories. Neil lives in the South West with his wife and children.

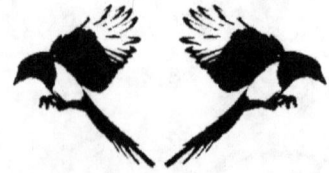